praise for SKIN ELEGIES

"Cinching bands of filmic narrative tighten. You must keep reading *Skin Elegies*, but why? Suspense. Meanwhile, take in the novel's rhythms, textual harmonics, and notion of human meaning lost/gained/lost in the multiverse—these also are its propellants. Its friable core is story. Lance Olsen's newest work is an amazing literary experiment."

—Stacey Levine, author of *The Girl with Brown Fur* and
My Horse and Other Stories

"Reading *Skin Elegies* feels like watching your mind explode, translating and transfiguring infinite possibilities into a brilliant galaxy all around and piercingly inside you. Memories spark and intensify, each flare fueled by compassion, invention, despair, horror. We are not ourselves, alone. Lance Olsen's spectacularly innovative novel is a song of exultation for the limitlessness of our minds—and a lament for the limits of our bodies."

—Melanie Rae Thon, author of *The 7th Man*

"Olsen takes the notion of the ghost in the machine to its superlative. Grappling with the human limits of and capacities for violence, grief, tragedy, and tenderness, *Skin Elegies* asks us to contemplate how the self is constructed and managed in and beyond the twenty-first century. A novel of kaleidoscopic horror—and Olsen at his most haunting."

—Lindsey Drager, author of *The Archive of Alternative Endings*

"*Skin Elegies* is the novel that the twenty-first century has been waiting for. Brilliantly conceived and impossible to sum up because it radiates in so many directions, it poignantly articulates the always-ever-present of the Now, relating experiences as disparate in time and space as John Lennon's murder, the plastic smell inside an astronaut's helmet, the consciousness of mountains. With the lyricism of poetry, its clouds of association conjure a theater of memory so profound and interconnected that we feel in our guts how the past, indeed, isn't really past. Which is another way of saying, the future is already here; it just isn't finished."

—Steve Tomasula, *VAS: An Opera in Flatland*

"Not since the revolutionary novels of Rudy Wurlitzer in the 1960s and 1970s have I encountered such a stunningly ambitious and astonishing narrative bricolage as Olsen's *Skin Elegies*. This meaty metanovel takes an esthetically and judiciously selected handful of our most vital history from 1945 to a prescient 2072, atomizes and digitizes it, then hits the SHUFFLE button before replaying the events through a set of hallucinogenic filters that Instagram would kill for. The effect is like riding a rollercoaster through a set of stargates, looping in an out of a multiverse composed of unforgettable characters and scintillant prose-poems. As fresh as the unfolding new decade, yet as eternal as the oneiric oracles of Tiresias, this book rebuilds our shared past and channels our mutual futures."

—Paul Di Filippo, author of *Ribofunk* and *Cosmocopia*

"Told through the metaphor of a mind upload technology that is almost certainly in our future, *Skin Elegies* simultaneously sets nine stories spiraling into each other, becoming the other, collapsing under their own weight and re-emerging as something new. Held together as much by the couple in the supercomputer and the nine other narrators as by the reader herself, Olsen boldly challenges us to recognize that our ability to create meaning in the present might just be what saves us."

—Jarret Middleton, author of *Darkansas*

"Visions erupt throughout this magnificent text, a twenty-first-century metamorphoses, an Ovid come back to restore us to awe. The comparison might make other writers quail, but not Lance Olsen, the

American most of the moment and farthest off the chain. Here he often works with figures from history, like the *Challenger* astronauts and the victims at Columbine, but even those who never made the headlines make bold and bruising new shapes of their stories. *Skin Elegies* shreds."

—John Domini, author of *Movieola!*

"The curiously soulful mosaic of *Skin Elegies*'s stories of connections missed, broken, catastrophic, and impossible is a reminder that, for all that has been and will be made of Olsen's architectonic innovations, his novels are never other than deeply humane and inspirited, not to mention pure pleasure for the adventurous reader. *Skin Elegies* is horrific, elegiac, far-seeing, and brilliant."

—Gabriel Blackwell, author of *CORRECTION* and *Babel*

SKIN ELEGIES

ALSO BY LANCE OLSEN

NOVELS
Live from Earth
Tonguing the Zeitgeist
Burnt
Time Famine
Freaknest
Girl Imagined by Chance
10:01
Nietzsche's Kisses
Anxious Pleasures
Head in Flames
Calendar of Regrets
Theories of Forgetting
There's No Place Like Time
Dreamlives of Debris
My Red Heaven

SHORT STORIES
My Dates with Franz
Scherzi, I Believe
Sewing Shut My Eyes
Hideous Beauties
How to Unfeel the Dead

NONFICTION
Ellipse of Uncertainty
Circus of the Mind in Motion
William Gibson
Lolita: A Janus Text
Rebel Yell: A Short Guide to Fiction Writing
Architectures of Possibility: After Innovative Writing
[[there.]]

SKIN
ELEGIES

— a novel —

LANCE OLSEN

DZANC
BOOKS

DZANC
BOOKS

5220 Dexter Ann Arbor Rd.
Ann Arbor, MI 48103
www.dzancbooks.org

First Edition: November 2021
Cover design by Matthew Revert
Interior design by Michelle Dotter

ISBN 9781950539352

Printed in the United States of America

10   9   8   7   6   5   4   3   2   1

for Andi,
& our timelessnesses

Tell me what you see vanishing and I
Will tell you who you are
　　　—W. S. Merwin

　　　　　　　　　　　Each moment is a place
　　　　　　　　　　　you've never been.
　　　　　　　　　　　　　—Mark Strand

Nobody wants to be here
and nobody wants to leave.
　　　—Cormac McCarthy

　　　　　　　　　　　We'll meet again
　　　　　　　　　　　Don't know where
　　　　　　　　　　　Don't know when
　　　　　　　　　　　But I know we'll meet again
　　　　　　　　　　　Some sunny day
　　　　　　　　　　　—Hughie Charles/Ross Parker

29 :::: october :::: 2072 :::: 11:12 a.m.

w   ca   u h   a—

ha

her

w   n't I   a

wh   n't I tou   er   a

why an't I tou   her   an

her ha

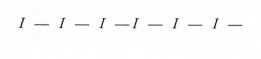

why can't

th

the

this—

11 :::: march :::: 2011

————————————————CH. 01

—is not for you.

It's for me.

You need to understand that.

I don't know you.
You have nothing to do with me.
You could be somebody else.
You could be anybody else.

29 :::: october :::: 1969

Music Opening: Chorus of "House of Memories" by Panic! At The Disco...

Ry: Hey, everybody. I'm Ry Himari. Welcome to another Random Access Memory podcast, coming to you indirect and unlive from the heart of Lotusland, located just between the downed hopes of Shaky Town and the communal hallucinations of our City of Angels, where, as the great Eduardo Galeano once remarked, history never really says *Goodbye,* just: *See you later.*

11 :::: march :::: 2011

Without you,
this story would be just
one more among
billions.

20 :::: april :::: 1999

—I can't—

2 :::: may :::: 1945

It's all hornets in the head now, isn't it? the little boy whispers.

8 :::: december :::: 1980

You were there—

20 :::: april :::: 1999

I can't place myself.

29 :::: october :::: 1969

Ry: Do I have a great episode for you today. Let me set the stage by taking you back to the temporal roil we sometimes refer to as 1969…

11 :::: march :::: 2011

——————————————CH. 02

This is the kind of
cell phone novel you read
every day on your commute
into Tokyo's marrow.

Except in this case
it isn't a novel.

You could
maybe call it
a trash diary.

Explanation—

8 :::: december :::: 1980

You were there, only nobody saw you.

11 :::: march :::: 2011

Explanation residue.

Think of me
as remembering out loud
for a little while
in the palm
of your hand.

20 :::: april :::: 1999

I was me a minute ago.

Weren't we?

11 :::: september :::: 2001

There may have been—there may be still, yes, look—a red ball suspended in midair; there may be beautiful children below—

8 :::: august :::: 1974

—was our hope—

2 :::: may :::: 1945

It's all hornets in the head now, isn't it? the little boy whispers. He's eight, I want to say, nine, kneeling beside me on the cement floor.

They've become the world. Yes.

Sound turned matter, offers the little boy.

You can see it. The noise—

What does it look like?

28 :::: january :::: 1986

[[
Flight deck, fore seats—
Commander: Dick Scobee
Pilot: Mike Smith

Flight deck, aft seats—
Mission Specialist: Ellison Onizuka
Mission Specialist: Judy Resnik

Mid-deck—
Mission Specialist: Ron McNair
Payload Specialist: Greg Jarvis
Payload Specialist: Christa McAuliffe
]]

20 :::: april :::: 1999

I was me a minute ago.

I was there.

I'm sure of it.

2 :::: may :::: 1945

What does it look like?

White static. How long will it—

Just a few seconds. That's all. It will feel endless, but it won't be. Go ahead. Tell me what happened.

10 :::: june :::: 2015

The day I turned nine was the day I became dust.

8 :::: august :::: 1974

Here was our holiness.

2 :::: may :::: 1945

Tell me what—

29 :::: october :::: 1969

Ry: Picture the cops in Newark, New Jersey, confiscating thirty thousand copies of John and Yoko's album *Two Virgins* because the photo of the couple in their birthday suits on the cover violated the state's pornography laws. Picture the first Boeing 747 rolling out of the company's new factory in Everett, Washington. Nixon ordering those secret bombing runs in Cambodia. James Earl Ray. Sirhan Sirhan. And Jim Morrison dropping his pants and exposing more than his dark soul on a Miami stage one March evening in front of ten thousand fans.

10 :::: june :::: 2015

Bombs began falling out of the afternoon sky.

This is Assad's gift for us, Mahmoud, my father said. Remember it. This is what he gives his people.

The day I turned nine was the day I saw the building next to mine turn into a tall flower of soot. I saw a hand lying in the street. I saw grown-ups running with towels to their faces, go down and get up again and keep running.

20 :::: april :::: 1999

I was there.

I'm sure of it.

And now I'm—

11 :::: march :::: 2011

————————————————CH. 03

I'm not a writer.

You probably already guessed that.

I teach math at a middle school
in Tomioka, a small ugly
oceanside town.

I taught math at a middle school
in Tomioka, a small ugly
oceanside town
in the Fukushima Prefecture.

For nearly fifteen years.

I grew up there.

Yet—these tenses.

What do you
do with all these tenses,
these continuous
misplacements in time?

28 :::: january :::: 1986

T - 106.000
Liquid oxygen vent cap withdrawn.

T - 105.000
Dick Scobee: *Goes the beanie cap.*

T - 104.000
Ellison Onizuka: *Doesn't it go the other way?*

(Laughter.)

T - 101.473
Mike Smith: *God, I hope not, Ellison.*

29 :::: october :::: 1969

Ry: *Monty Python's Flying Circus. Tommy* and *Midnight Cowboy.* The Stonewall Rebellion and the Manson murders. Woodstock and Altamont. *Abbey Road* and *The Velvet Underground.* Levi's first pair of bell-bottom jeans, that last awesome installment of the original *Star Trek* series, and Neil Armstrong bouncing slo-mo across the lunar desert.

2 :::: may :::: 1945

Just a few seconds, the eight-year-old boy whispers. The eight-or-nine-year-old boy whispers. *That's all. It will feel endless, but it won't be. Go ahead. Tell me what happened. You broke out southeast with your wife and the officers.*

My officers. And my wife and brother-in-law. Yes.

It was late.

Past midnight. We hadn't slept in three days. Two. Three. Time had become adrenalized, hazy. It was like looking at the sun through a dirty window.

It took your column quite a—

Forty-five minutes. The Soviets were everywhere, fanning out through Berlin from the north. The air was choked with oily smoke from the fires across the city. There was no electricity. There were no gas lamps. The infrastructure was gone. We thought we could use the darkness to our advantage.

You were surprised to see others on the streets, too.

We didn't expect to come across so many civilians. They were loitering in front of ruined apartment blocks. You could see it in their eyes, how unnatural fear and reality felt. Everybody had become a believer.

10 :::: june :::: 2015

I saw a woman's hand lying in the street.

That evening grown-ups stood in front of ruined apartment blocks, windows smashed, walls missing, tattered clothing mixed with heaps of debris everywhere.

They were trying to understand. You could see it in their eyes. Everything felt still and far away. A man covered in grime sat on the sidewalk. He held his face in his palms. His white shirt was spattered with blood. He was bleeding from his ears.

I knew it was a woman's hand because of the red fingernail polish.

I knew because it was still holding a small purse.

You could see into people's living rooms through the blown-out walls. They were sitting in circles on rugs, legs crossed, covered in white powder, trying to take in what had just happened to them.

Nothing in my life ever felt more believable.

God never felt so close.

8 :::: august :::: 1974

Here was our holiness: cellular amplification.

Who doesn't dream about the fervor of network?

About the shattering of dishes?

That kind of opacity?

That dense entanglement?

We wanted the weight of abundance. We wanted two tongues, one mind. We wanted four legs stomping, four hands tightening their love.

11 :::: september :::: 2001

There may have been—there may be still, yes, look—a red ball suspended in midair; there may be beautiful children below, every face a different shade of brown, frozen in mid-run, midgame; there may still be a pale blue sheet stopped in mid-flutter on the clothesline behind them, flanked by a family of shockingly white socks, white boxers, white panties, white brassieres, white handkerchiefs; each child may be elated, secretly sorrowful, worried about what others are thinking, absorbed with nothing except that red ball fixed above his or her head in the pallid afternoon sky; they may have formed a semi-circle; some may be singing to themselves, although Professor Johnson—Ryana—

8 :::: august :::: 1974

Here was our hope: remain a fraction.
That paradise of connection.
That awe of inclusion.
We wanted the volume louder.
We wanted the mob scene positively unglued.

20 :::: april :::: 1999

And now we—

I—

He was himself a minute ago. Ourselves. Let's call
us Dave. That's what everyone else—

Dave Sanders.

We were there.

Dave were.

Let's call *there* a long corridor the color of sameness.
Let's call it a long hall the color of sameness in a high
school the color of very tired. Let's call it a second-floor
hall and call that the setting.

That's where everything flies apart.

All the minutes.

All the there.

And now Dave are—

Where are Dave?

8 :::: december :::: 1980

You were there, only nobody saw you. This is what you are good at: not being there when you are there. This is what people are bad at: seeing—giving a shit about any part of the universe that isn't them. Everything has become yoga classes for middle-brow midlife worker bees craving a weekly application of Eastern clichés to their washed-out existences to encourage them to stop caring, stop thinking, stop living. Because you grow up and all the lights go off one by one and then it's Olivia Newton-John. It's Captain and Tennille and your life dimming out of view before you. Because later it will be something else. Later it will be this skinny balding doctor standing in a puddle of blood in a mob scene emergency room, cracking open a guy's blown-apart chest, plunging in his hands, lifting out the heart, holding it in his palms, feeling the—the—what do you call it?

11 :::: march :::: 2011

—————————————————CH. 04

I wonder
if you can appreciate
when I tell you
I loved my students
but never liked them
very much.

20 :::: april :::: 1999

> Let's call it the weight of abundance: a gray forest frantic with bird chatter. Except there aren't any trees. There isn't any sky. There isn't any ground. Except it isn't a forest and the bird chatter isn't bird chatter and sometimes Dave hearing heavy thunder in our chest.

28 :::: january :::: 1986

T - 93.000
Judy Resnik: *Got your harnesses locked?*

T - 92.000
Mike Smith: *What for?*

(Laughter.)

T - 89.000
Dick Scobee: *I won't lock mine. I might have to reach for something.*

T - 88.000
Mike Smith: *Oohkaaaay.*

T - 84.320
Christa McAuliffe: ...

T - 74.202

Mike Smith closes his eyes to savor the bitter scent of plastics and warm electronics inside his helmet. Here it is, he thinks: what life should smell like, always.

11 :::: september :::: 2001

Except I can't be sure. Perhaps the children are listening to the song whistled by that giant with three fingers missing on his left hand—a father—hers—ours—Ryana's—clattering in the shabby shed at the edge of the dead-grass yard, beyond which unfurls a hundred flat humid acres of rickety barn, muddy pond, cotton and corn, the scent of hay and gasoline-soaked rags in the hot breeze. It may be the intensity of the sunlight that makes those children squint, captures them in mid-plunge, blind and oblivious, yet I—I can't quite—yet the professor—Ryana—senses the children's world as increasingly gauzy and weightless as she wades farther into the warm dark sea, up to her ankles, up to her knees.

11 :::: march :::: 2011

Because my students
were the most
distracted,
fidgety,
self-conscious,
exposed,
alarmed
creatures on earth.

In the end they believed
everything was all about them.

They expected everything
would be all about them forever.

They made their naiveté
and self-importance
into a blunt weapon.

People like me were
simply poor stand-ins for
their gaming consoles—
except we possessed
the ability to grade
their work
and thereby
ruin their futures.

Once in a while they
may have even liked me.

How can a teacher
ever tell, really?

20 :::: april :::: 1999

What we can tell is this.

This is what we believe we can tell.

Floating through that gray forest that isn't one, we find memories accumulating here and there like dust bunnies. If they are memories, and not something else. Misunderstandings, say. Hope clusters.

Because Dave are walking toward the cafeteria.

It is the blah of a hazy Tuesday.

It is the monotone of 11:30.

We recall this distinctly.

And then there is no then.

No there.

We could go into details.

Except there aren't any.

29 :::: october :::: 1969

Ry: Now picture something equally momentous transpiring completely below radar in this cramped computer lab in the basement of this
nondescript building on the UCLA campus and one just like it at the
Stanford Research Institute. It's 10:30 in the p.m., October 29, 1969,
and these two guys just reach out, flip a switch and ... and the *Internet*
comes to life. Nothing less than our communal hallucinations, our
collective mind uploaded, that infinitely complex, almost incomprehensibly networked digital ectoplasm we find ourselves adrift in every
single day snaps on as if it has been there all along and ... and virtually
nobody even notices. And those two guys? A grad student and a pro-
grammer I'll put some money on you've never heard of: Charley Kline
and Bill Duvall. We just happen to be fortunate enough to have none
other than the former as our guest today. Thanks so much for joining
us on Random Access Memory, Charley.

8 :::: december :::: 1980

Only now it was just this chubby, clean-shaven, double-chinned,
twenty-five-year-old in a pair of oversized aviator glasses and fur hat
and overcoat with fur collar. It was you. Let's call him you. It was
how you loitered on the sidewalk on West Seventy-Second Street out
front of the Dakota. Scarf. Jeans. Track shoes. *Double Fantasy* album
hugged to your chest. You wore a red T-shirt with some oriental crap
written across it in black and nobody saw you strike up a conversation with the doorman, with José, with José Perdomo from Cuba,
the man with glasses big as a scuba mask. Nobody saw you hang out
with him on and off throughout the day, shooting the breeze in front
of his gold-painted guard booth next to the gothic archway that led

into whatever it led into. You and José commented about how warm the weather was for December, how it wasn't what it used to be, how everything was changing, how it always would be, look at these temperatures, look at these dismays. You asked him where you could get a good cup of coffee around there that didn't cost a million bucks. Then you asked him where he was without looking too interested in José's answer. It was just a question. It was just a way to pass another minute. José told you at a nearby barbershop getting a Teddy Boy in preparation for a photoshoot with Annie Leibovitz who would be dropping by soon, which is you pay attention, which is you're not done falling yet, you can tell some of the lights are still on, which is you learned some stuff about José and then you forgot it because it didn't matter, and fans came and went, nobodies busy not noticing you. Because later it will be something else. Later it will be that *Rolling Stone* cover with him, naked and fetal, clinging in their bed to Yoko all dressed in black. Only now it was this dumpy dumbass with camera and Hitler mustache walking up to you and asking if you were waiting for him, too. We're all waiting for him, you said. The dumpy dumbass with camera and Hitler mustache said he was from New Jersey in a tone that suggested his words were a secret language in which every syllable meant something more than it meant to mean. He said he'd dropped off his copy of *A Spaniard in the Works* yesterday to get signed and was back to pick it up. He must have thought you two had become best friends. I'm from Hawaii, you said, using his system of communication. He said: Where are you staying while you're in town? You said: Why the fuck do *you* want to know? He looked at you, sizing you up, replied: Go back to where you were standing and leave me the fuck alone.

11 :::: march :::: 2011

—————————————————————CH. 05

Because when I
was a child,
my fisherman father
used to take me out
on his boat,
just the two of us.

These are my happiest memories.

The amazing accomplishment
of his sun-rumpled face.

The way he had
of brushing his short thin hair
straight forward to cover
all he was rapidly losing.

He somehow reminded me
of a beautiful
wrinkled cotton shirt.

He wanted his daughter
to see what he saw,
take pleasure
in what gave him pleasure.

The wave chop.

The briny spray.

We couldn't stop
beaming as we briefly
became the same person.

*The child of a frog
is a frog,* he used to say,
and we would laugh
and laugh at us.

8 :::: august :::: 1974

Because when The Me of Us was a child, The Father of Us carpooled to
ballet every Saturday morning through the wooded hills and existential
nutrient deficiency of Corning, New York.

He waited to comb out our hair in front of the others gathered
in tutus and rivalry. The Father of Us shaped our pigtails. Smartened
our tiara. Primped us before the mothers so that we might absorb their
admiration and envy.

What a dad, they said.

What a guy.

2 :::: may :::: 1945

Which is when the breakout—it didn't—

We took shelter in the Schultheiß brewery.

Where the hornets live.

Yes.

You led your wife and your brother-in-law inside, down into the cellar. And you told them—what did you tell them, Erich?

No, no, Lieutenant Rücker, I said. Don't even— *Back. Farther. Farther.* Against the wall. That's it. Don't even think about— Hands out of your pockets. *Now.* Good. That's good. Thank you. Make no mistake. Military protocol will remain in effect until the— Let me just catch— Isn't it— Isn't it extraordinary that this whole joke has boiled down to a single windowless room?

What was his name?

Whose?

Your brother-in-law's. His given name.

I—

You don't remember, do you.

It will come to me.

Go on.

Can you feel it? I asked them. It's like— It's like we're still accelerating. The burning structures fluttering past. The future rushing in. But don't— I know what I'm doing. I'm— What? Yes. Me neither. Thirty.

Thirty. Look at me. Youngest general in the entire Reich. If one can call it that. If one can— I suppose we're all a little tired tonight. This morning. But let me assure you: I know what I'm about. You want to— Of course you do, Lieutenant Rücker. Who wouldn't? It will feel— For an instant it will feel like what watching a lightning storm looks like. And then you will understand, just for this blazing fraction, that firing a pistol is like holding hands with God.

11 :::: september :::: 2001

Only now it—

10 :::: june :::: 2015

—next morning—

11 :::: march :::: 2011

——————————————CH. 06

> *It will always be dark*
> *one inch ahead of you, Himari,*
> my mother used to tell me,
> propping me up
> after I took a tumble.
> *Fall down seven times,*
> *stand up eight.*

She used to tell me:
Himari, don't forget:
Not seeing is a flower.

11 :::: september :::: 2001

Only now it is Doctor Dressler arriving at 3:05, knees creaky, spine tight, hair assertively unkempt, a thick graywhite outburst crowning his head, strolling up the path to the Jade Villa past the last flowers of the season, red gerbera, lilac lupin, the wall phone having jangled him awake from his after-lunch nap, tabby Timo bounding resentfully off his tummy at the intrusion, news from New York beginning to arrive over the radio on the drive—the plane, the World Trade Center, what a terrible accident, what a terrible shame. Doctor Dressler had packed his physician's bag this morning, knowing the call would be coming, if not when. It was something he had gotten used to never getting used to. He awoke to find Timo grouchy, back hunched against him on the windowsill, and his wife, Ry, nowhere to be found. She was— Where was Ry? Shopping, he seems to recall now, or was it off to enjoy friends over coffee and cake at a cozy café in Old Town? Before stepping out himself, Doctor Dressler left her a note on the kitchen countertop, black marker on yellow lined paper: *Suicide. Back by 7:00. Love, Max.*

10 :::: june :::: 2015

What was hardest to accept was next morning the clocks kept collecting the minutes inside them just like usual.

There was no school that day and the day after more bombs fell.

A corner of our hospital went away.

Part of the market.

My mother stopped talking. My little sister Ana, too. She wrapped her arms around my mother's legs and refused to let go, moving through our house like this, my mother and her one body, one mind.

When my father took Ana by the shoulders to try to gently pry her off, my little sister shut her eyes tight and shook her head *no-no-no* and kept holding on hard as she could.

28 :::: january :::: 1986

T - 59.000

Dick Scobee: *One minute downstairs.*

T - 50.297

Ron McNair: [[... is what I want my sax solo to sound like when ... second brother in orbit ... first music played live in weightlessness three hundred miles above sea level ... last track on Jean-Michel Jarre's *Rendez-Vous* ... and it's going to be beautiful, man ... this pure primal point ...]]

T - 40.000

Mike Smith: *Ullage pressures are up.*

29 :::: october :::: 1969

Ry: Thanks so much for joining us on Random Access Memory. I'm delighted to have you up to my studio-in-quotation-marks, Charley. What an amazing tale you were part of.

Charley: Actually—thanks for inviting me, Ry—actually it didn't feel all that amazing. It just felt like one story among billions. That's the thing a lot of people find weird. Bill and I— We had no idea what we were doing. Seriously. We had a bunch of programming assignments we needed to complete that night. That's all. We got to this one, blew it, tweaked some stuff, everything seemed to work fine, and we checked it off our list and moved on to the next one. I'm guessing it took less than an hour.

Ry: And you were ... what? Twenty-five? Twenty-six?

Charley: Twenty-one.

Ry: When you're inside a tale like that, it never feels like you're inside a tale like that.

Charley: It just felt like we were ... you know ... doing stuff before we did other stuff. Like—what do you call it?

8 :::: august :::: 1974

Sin. When The Father of Us snapped his fingers, our little sister Ashley and The Me of Us knew right away sin had entered our house. We took our spots, kneeled, noses to living room wall, hands behind heads, anticipating.

Sometimes we remained that way for hours. Sometimes the sheer voltage of the pose satisfied him. Sometimes we heard the belt slide out of its loops.

Sometimes that was all.

Sometimes it wasn't.

Sometimes it was hard to walk straight for half a week because of the raw, the red, the greenpurple blotches of error across our butts, down our thighs.

There were occasions we didn't understand what we had done. It didn't matter. The essential thing was to accept we were cupped in his palms. The Father of Us was doing his daughters a favor. He was teaching us, shaking us gently out of our drowsiness.

Lavishing upon us a competition of surprises that enlivened the flames in our brainpans.

8 :::: december :::: 1980

Which if you think about it every person really only has one story to tell, and you're not from Hawaii, not in any way that counts, which is you didn't grow up in a whatever suburb of Atlanta, even though you did. Your dad wasn't an asshole in the Air Force who watched Lawrence Welk from his recliner, listening to dead accordion noises while chucking Hot Tamales into his mouth, even though he was, even though he did. You never saw the purple marks like hickeys he left behind on your mom's neck when she got out of line, which you did, which is it happens, because women. The one story you have to tell is the power you gained when you were seven over the little people living in the walls of your bedroom. Only it could have been others. It could have been, say, Johnny Carson or Elizabeth Taylor. It could have been Bowie. It could have been them, you thought about it, you considered, only it was something else, because John, because in high school the little people started asking you what the big deal was about ditching classes, whispering to you about how all your teachers were idiots or they wouldn't be teachers, how everyone knew they taught Faulkner from the CliffsNotes. You could smell it on their chintzy sports coats, their dead-lung dresses. The little people gave you the codes, told you to become a garbage head because they had to eat to reproduce, and the more little people, the more interesting thoughts you would have, so zoomers and buttons and blue boys and we were The Egg Man, which was proof how alike you and him were, how easy it was when you were fifteen to live out on the streets for two weeks, see how they fly, before Jesus crashed into your life, shouting at the top of his rage *Fuck the fucking little people and get into my goddamned heart*, and all the lights crashed on again, you precipitously realizing the older somebody gets, the stupider somebody gets, because those lights then start going off, and how can anybody believe in Himalayan salt lamps and all the other mind-control tapeworms fastened to your intestinal walls? That's the only real story, which is why you began working at the South DeKalb County YMCA day camp and in Arkansas at Fort Chaffee with those kids, those refugee kids from Vietnam, because you could see in them how Jesus loved each and every one of us in his own unique fucked-up way, all that cellular amplification, all that holy-holy bonfire, you had to squint because there was so goddamned much light leaking out of them. You played your guitar, led them in singalongs by reporting wisdom the little people visited upon you, one voice, one mind, one bind, because I am he as you are he, you took the shy ones aside and showed them how to shoot arrows and feel hopeless. When somebody tired out on a hike, you hoisted him onto your back and carried him down into camp, just like Jesus did in whatever part of the Bible it was, so it didn't matter that you failed at college or. What mattered was those kids kept growing up into who they weren't. It killed you, watching all those lights winking off one by one simply because they started listening to Kenny Rogers. It tore your freaking heart out, and the only thing left to do at some point was book a flight to Hawaii, throw away your last money at the ritziest hotels, drive your rental to an overlook at sunset, sky above you one big Glory-be-unto-Him-in-the-Highest carnage, attach a hose to the exhaust pipe, and roll up the windows, because—

11 :::: march :::: 2011

> Because these continuous
> misplacements in time.
>
> They are like
> helium in your fist.

29 :::: october :::: 1969

Charley: Because my professor—Len Kleinrock—Len asked me to see if I could figure out how to send a simple transmission over ARPANET.

Ry: ARPANET?

Charley: Advanced Research Projects Agency Network—the first data-transmission system. Originally funded by the Department of Defense. Which, by the way, is how that myth got started about the military developing the Internet as a way of maintaining communications after a nuclear strike. Anyway, Len Kleinrock—

Ry: One of the developers of ARPANET—

Charley: Len had pioneered the mathematical theory of packet networks. Being part of the ARPANET project gave him the opportunity to test his ideas.

Ry: Because there was this big problem with the concept of networking at the time.

Charley: Back in the day computers couldn't talk to each other. Wes Clark—this guy at MIT—Wes came up with a solution. He built a machine that incompatible computers could connect to each other through. Each would only have to work out how to exchange information with this gizmo, which was called a switch. And the switch we used was called an IMP—Interface Message Processor. UCLA got the first one, the Stanford Research Institute the second.

Ry: Switches developed into what we call routers—translators, like, for computers that spoke different languages.

Charley: The idea was to connect ours in LA to Bill's about 350 miles north. You think router these days, and you think this little contraption that sits under your desk. Only these IMPs were the size of refrigerators.

Ry: So tell us what happened.

11 :::: march :::: 2011

————————————————————————————CH. 07

My lunchbreak
was over and I was
in my classroom.

It was a Friday afternoon,
almost three o'clock,
the day overcast and chilly.

My students were restless,

ready to move on
to their extracurricular clubs
or enjoy the beginning
of whatever they thought of
when they thought of
their weekends.

I was ready to spend
another hour or two
trying to help the slow ones
who couldn't be helped,
then go home and listen
to Miles Davis,
maybe Coltrane,
not-thinking on my couch,
pleasantly brain dead,
beer in my hand,
bowl of ramen
in my lap.

I remember distinctly
standing there at the front
of the classroom,
marker raised,
pronouncing the words
linear functions—

—and next—

—well, you already know
what happens next.

29 :::: october :::: 1969

Charley: I was sitting in the computer lab in the basement of Boelter Hall, picking at this bowl of ramen in my lap around ten at night. Someone had painted the walls this horrendous lime green. Everything smelled like warm electronics. I was working at a terminal that looked like a cross between a typewriter and a fax machine. It was connected to our IMP. The IMP was connected to our host computer, an SDS Sigma 7—one of those whales that used tons of power and came with under-floor air conditioning to prevent it from overheating, which it always wanted to do.

28 :::: january :::: 1986

T - 37.673

A punch in the heart, and behind Mike Smith's forehead it is 1972. It is the cockpit of his A-6 Intruder lifting off the deck of the Kitty Hawk, Gulf of Tonkin dropping away below, sky like the future rushing in. It is Operation Linebacker, the bombing run designed to slow transportation of supplies flooding in from the North. It is this tearing through the cloud layer, this bursting into sudden hazy graybl—

8 :::: december :::: 1980

Which is—which is when that fisherman started tapping at your car window, asking if you were okay, and you opened your eyes to see Jesus in his baggy aloha shirt smiling down upon you, insane beard, sun-staring visionary eyes, surrounded by all these post-nuclear rays, mouthing his words of gentle mercy: *You fucking retard—you can't even do this right, can you?,* which is when you awoke a second time, your new life beginning in Castle Memorial Hospital, peering up into the faces of that circle of doctors peering down at you, you in mid-explanation about how you had come to conceive of yourself lately as a boxer in the twenty-seventh round, while Christ whispered tenderly into your soul: *You little shit—I TOLD you to fuck the little people and get into my goddamned affection … what are you, some kind of one-man Watergate for spiritual cripples? Stand the fuck up, dust yourself off, and let me help you save your sorry ass, you little bitch,* and that became the one story, the only story, the story you had to tell yourself for the rest of your days, which is how you didn't talk your way into staying on at that hospital as an employee, even though you did, working in the print shop in the basement with these horrendous lime-green walls, because there you could be alone with Our Savior and one day fall head over heels for a celestial spirit named Gloria Hiroko, the travel agent you visited once when contemplating a trip around the world, because Gloria looked just like *her* on that album cover you were clutching to your chest outside the Dakota, and she let you join Jesus in her heart, despite the lack of room at the time, despite it being like trying to squirm your whole body into a raisin, which is you could tell from the start Gloria would forgive anything you were capable of, cherish you despite the you of you. You didn't soon after that get into a shouting match with some hogbeast nurse sporting loose arm fat, even though you did, quit your job on the spot, even though and so forth, and thus the Resurrection and the Life came unto you and spake softly, filled with His magnificent whatever, whispering: *There are worse things to become than a pathetic-shit night security guard who spends every day adding a drop too much kirsch to the fondue, and sometimes you've just got to hit them, sure, nothing dramatic, the sky won't fall or anything, you'll see, just a clap on the ear, peck with the open hand, enough to make them take notice and sit down and consider for a minute who they really are, what*

they're really worth, wake them into an unpacked newness, because Gloria
will absolve you and in the end allow you to stay home while she goes out to
earn some bread, amen, just like she *allowed* ~~him~~ *to stay home and become*
a phantom for those five years, no interviews, no records, you sitting naked
in the middle of your living room, earphones on, listening to their albums
with the volume turned way up, because happiness IS *a warm gun, moth-*
erfucker, yes it is—hatching your plans to evolve into a what-do-you-call-it
human being, which is to say: Look how many men have been precisely
as troubled morally and spiritually as you. Some of them kept records.
Now you've got one, too, and you will offer it to others, and maybe
someday, Alpha and Omega willing, someone will even take something
meaningful away from it, hallelujah.

8 :::: august :::: 1974

What The Me of Us means to say is this: Do you know that feeling
you get when you're reading a story and you come across a thought or
emotion which until that very instant you believed you were the only
person ever to have experienced?

Then there you are, all cuddled beneath your quilt on the living
room sofa, getting it that somebody else somewhere else—somebody
who may have already been dead hundreds of years before you were
even born; somebody in Tbilisi or Topeka—has had that exact same
thought, that exact same emotion?

It is as if that person has just reached out and taken your hand.

This is what being the fraction of our father feels like.

Every inhalation.

Every exhalation.

Every punch in the heart.

29 :::: october :::: 1969

Ry: So the tale goes you were the guy who developed the software in order for your operating system to transmit stuff, except there was no one to transmit stuff to.

Charley: Until that point, all I could do was send data back and forth to myself. Then, like I say, Stanford got their IMP connected to their host computer, an SDS 940. Bill and I decided the simplest thing would be to use a terminal on my computer to log in to the system on his.

Ry: Only things didn't go exactly as planned.

11 :::: september :::: 2001

Because, ecologist and botanist both, Ryana had specialized in climate change at Rice University long before *climate change* was what you called it, not a hundred miles from where she had grown up on that farm under that muggy pallid sky outside Ganado, Texas. Her focus was on the relationship between overpopulation—roughly 1.8 billion bodies the year she was born, 6.2 billion today, ninety-two years later, and from here on out one inconceivable projection after another: 8.6 in 2030, 11.2 by the turn of the century ... even though ten billion is the uppermost limit the planet can in fact bear of us—the relationship between overpopulation and ever-diminishing resources, ever-rising prices, ever-increasing pollution, ever more political instability managed by ever more authoritarian regimes. Ryana's resources have been diminishing continuously, too. She noticed her eyesight slackening over the past six years, over the past two her ability to move. A walker materialized beneath her. Her university, where she maintained an office as professor emerita, began to raise concerns about her safety, her commute into her department.

28 ::::: january ::::: 1986

T - 34.000
—grayblueness and—

10 ::::: june ::::: 2015

Two weeks later we—

2 ::::: may ::::: 1945

And your wife—what was her name?

My wife? Was I—

What was your wife's name, Erich?

8 ::::: august ::::: 1974

The hardware. The software. The berserk number storms.

10 :::: june :::: 2015

—weeks later we—

28 :::: january :::: 1986

T - 34.000
Mike Smith: *Right engine helium tank is a little bit low.*

T - 32.000
Dick Scobee: *It was yesterday, too.*

T - 31.000
Mike Smith: *Okay.*

T - 30.000
Dick Scobee: *Thirty seconds down there.*

2 :::: may :::: 1945

What was your wife's name, Erich?

10 :::: june :::: 2015

Two weeks later we were in Alexandria.
    We did not start a new life there.

This is what people will tell you. They will say: We fled our homeland because of the war and started a new life in a new country. But it is not like that. What it is like is you begin to live between two lives. You are not here and you are not there. You are not then and you are not now. You are not you and you are not somebody else.

Living this way feels gray, like when you cannot sleep for days in a row because of the roar of explosions.

Cluster bombs.

Barrel bombs.

Bunker busters.

We did not know any of these words.
And then we did.

29 :::: october :::: 2072 :::: 10:30 a.m.

I'm delighted to welcome you this morning—my morning, at least—to the Mind Emulation Studies Department at Cairo University. My name is Riyana Arafa. I'm a computer neurologist and chair of our program. How pleased I am to see my hologram reaching—let me just—yes—nearly thirty thousand specialists, potential investors, and influencers at other universities and in corporate headquarters and media nodes around the—

29 :::: october :::: 1969

Interlude Music: 10 seconds: Chorus of "Computer Love" by Kraftwerk, fading in, fading out …

Ry: Again, everyone, I'm Ry Himari, this is the Random Access Memory podcast, and today I'm delighted to be speaking with digital revolutionary Charley Kline. Thanks for listening.

11 :::: september :::: 2001

"Computer Love"? Doctor Dressler finds himself trying to remember the song's title as he detonates through the front doors of the Jade Villa into staggering white sunlight, sensing it create him as he releases a pleasant hello for his nurse, who must be around here somewhere. Underfed, unflappable, thirty-five going on fifty, Anna has the sound system cranked up way too loud again. Doctor Dressler will have to speak with her about that. He rubs his cheek and the lyrics flourish within him: *I call this number for a data date. I don't know what to do. I need a rendezvous.* A small puff of pride, and Anna emerges from the kitchen, saying: *Did you hear? There is a second plane.*

8 :::: august :::: 1974

The Father of Us became a flight engineer.

Who wouldn't want to become one just like him?

We yearned after the hypotheses, the crystalline faultlessness of syllogistics.

The hardware. The software. The berserk number storms.

Even as The Father of Us taught us to see how ugly The Mother was, how self-centered, precarious, what a failure in a multitude of ways.

How could we ever repay him?

Ever thank him enough for his generosity?

He pointed out each of her faults in attentive detail, sometimes behind her back, sometimes to her face, so we could come to discern and number them as well.

How she could never pour without splashing. Never apply makeup without embarrassing. How she slept less and less, often only an hour or two each night, then tornadoed through our days.

Furious became her favorite color.

Once she disordered up to her room and slammed the door in a rage. At intervals she opened it, screamed blackness down upon us, slammed it once more. We continued to watch TV stoically. She repeated the gesture until the doorframe cracked, splintered, until she had broken our evening.

She was backaches.

Migraines, meanness, shadow-filled rooms.

She was a whirlwind of feigned glee and unfathomable grief.

2 :::: may :::: 1945

I— I can't seem to remember. How is that—

Your life is already beginning to forget you. This is how it happens, Erich. Your wife moved off to a corner in the room while you were speaking to your brother-in-law, didn't she. Slid down the wall, brought her knees up to her chest, rested her chin on them, hugged them close against her. She had lost her sense of decorum. She wasn't doing anything other than staring into the next few seconds.

Yes. I see her. Her name was—

And you told her—

Stop it, I told her. Please. Stop crying, my love. Try to control yourself. You're butchering what's left of my brain. Do you see your brother crying? Of course not. There is nothing to cry about. We have done what we could. We need to shore up our dignity for one last push. Would you care for a Jew cigarette? Eckstein. They certainly knew their cigarettes. If nothing else. You have to— *I told you to stop moving, Lieutenant Rücker.* Thank you. Both of you. You have my word. Everything is going to be just—

20 :::: april :::: 1999

—just Dave lazying toward the cafeteria for his lunchbreak, when he is still an is, hands in pockets as old philosophers in Basel and middle-aged girls' basketball coaches in Colorado do, when the first guesses erupt from the parking lot.

We had no idea what they meant.

Except our legs have already become running.

Our legs-become-running are joined by the running legs of two janitors, Rich and Rob.

We stop long enough to watch our hand—Dave's hand—pull the fire alarm. We stop long enough to listen to our mouth fill with sound objects. The sound objects direct the students in various stages of metabolism—a hundred, a hundred fifty—to sprint toward life because—

11 :::: march :::: 2011

—————————————CH. 08

Because:
*A painting is
music you can see,*
Miles once said,
*and music is
a painting you can hear.*

Imagine being able
to encounter life
like that.

28 :::: january :::: 1986

T - 28.503
A punch in the heart, and behind Ellison Onizuka's forehead it is 1952. It is his parents' house in Kealakekua, Hawaii. It is Ellison, six, lying in damp grass out back at night, looking up into the no-light strewn with

stars, wondering precisely how far he would have to stretch in order to touch that awe above him.

11 :::: september :::: 2001

Only next it was Ryana finding herself steering her car through her final errands, performing her final role in her treasured diversion at the local theater company. She tried working out of her bungalow west of Rice, but it just wasn't the same. She missed bumping into her colleagues in the hall, striking up amicable exchanges about very little in order, simply, to take pleasure in their presence. She knew they had begun letting go of her, releasing her into the temporal haze of their pasts, not out of any sort of hardheartedness (they enjoyed her company, she was sure of it, enjoyed her banter, intelligence, buoyancy), but because they had more immediate matters to attend to. There was always the next committee meeting, administrative responsibility, class. Ryana understood this. Of course she did. Still, she could feel herself disappearing from their awareness a few cells at a time. Ryana Johnson was evaporating. That's how she thought of it. And then last month she became disoriented on her way to the bathroom at night, tripped, and somehow comically, ludicrously, awfully wedged herself between wall and bed. How could she have let such a thing happen? How in the world could she not extricate herself? How could her muscles have— She called out for help intermittently, pacing her energy, until the following afternoon the mailman heard her as he stepped onto the stoop. That evening she began packing up her books. When she needed a break, she surfed the Web. Within a week she was in touch with a nice doctor sporting a lovely Germanic accent in Basel.

10 :::: june :::: 2015

Within a week my father taught me how to deliver bread. This is how we made our living in Egypt. I felt like the man of the house when I was helping him.

Only the authorities said I could not go to school.

The other kids' parents told them to stop playing with me because I was from Syria. When they saw me outside, they ran after me. They made fun of me, hitting, calling me the son of a shoe. They trotted alongside me, calling me a faggot.

I made myself not cry.

I made myself run fast as I could.

Soon I did not go outside anymore.

Tell me: What was outside?

After I finished helping him every day, my father rewarded me by letting me use his cell phone for half an hour. I spent every minute looking at photographs and YouTube videos of Europe.

My mother saw what I was doing and told me I was wasting my time.

There is nothing for us there, she said.

She said: If you live in Europe you are already as good as dead.

I saw something else. I saw how in Germany crowds welcomed refugees at the train stations with smiles and clapping and candy. I saw how the supermarket shelves were so full of colorful food it made you giddy. Shiny cars rolled through tree-lined streets and every TV offered an infinite number of channels.

Everybody owned a laptop.

Everybody listened to the music they called schlager.

Men stood on sidewalks, kissing.

Sometimes I wondered why people are happier seeing two men holding guns than holding hands.

Even after a war, people will still be kissing and holding hands.

11 :::: march :::: 2011

—————————————————CH. 09

One night three years ago,
nearly ninety, frail,
increasingly diaphanous,
my father became disoriented
and fell on his way to the bathroom.

He hollered
for my mother
to help him.

Trying to wrestle
him from the floor
she had her stroke.

After that it was
difficult for her
to find sentences,
as if she had misplaced
them somewhere
inside herself.

Though she knew
what she wanted to say,
she could no longer
bring to her lips
the right words
in the right order.

It would take her
the longest time
to weave together
the shortest phrase.

My father, impatient,
ashamed of her,
angry, too, because
part of her had
left him for good,
would wait several seconds,
then step in to speak for her.

No, she would say
in the sweetest voice
when he was done.

Smiling,
teeth blotched brown,
my slight,
my fragile,
my tenacious mother:
No, dear, that's not it.

8 :::: august :::: 1974

One Christmas morning we padded out of our rooms in our furry
pink bunny-rabbit pajamas to discover The Mother planting presents
around the tree.

The Me of Us immediately assumed she was stealing them for herself and heaved into aghast pules.

Ashley trotted out to see what the cataclysm was about, saw us undone, and reflexively joined our conflagration.

The Father of Us appeared on the staircase, tying his robe shut, running his fingers through his still-flabbergasted hair, sizing up the situation collapsing into itself below.

Well, he said, she *is* capable of anything, isn't she?

28 ::::: january ::::: 1986

T - 12.000

CNN correspondent Tom Mintier: *Let's go down to the Kennedy Space Center now and take a look at Challenger sitting on its launch pad and—*

T - 10.000

Launch Commentator: *ten ...*

T - 9.000

Launch Commentator: *... nine ...*

T - 6.000

Dick Scobee: *There they go guys. Three at a hundred.*

T - 5.000

Launch Commentator: *... we have main engines start ...*

T - 4.883

Christa McAuliffe tries to rotate in her seat just enough to catch a glimpse of the single small porthole in the hatch far to her left on the mid-deck, somewhere beyond Greg Jarvis's pale blue spacesuit bulk, Ron McNair's, but the edge of her helmet keeps getting in the way.

T - 4.000
Launch Commentator: ... *four* ...

T - 3.000
Launch Commentator: ... *three* ...

T - 2.000
Launch Commentator: ... *two* ...

T - 1.000
Launch Commentator: ... *one* ...

T + .003
Judy Resnik: *All right.*

8 :::: december :::: 1980

What you're talking about here—it stands beyond education. It's a category of purity, which is everything matters. You can feel the molecules gathering mass around them—your flight to Atlanta, your purchase of those hollow-point bullets, your target practice in the woods on the fringes of the city, your flight to New York, how you spent Saturday, Sunday, today drifting alongside Holden Caulfield's paperback shadow, the Naumburg Bandshell in Central Park, the Carousel, because Jesus had led you to that article in *Esquire*, the one by Laurence Shames, about how John had entered that half decade of phantomhood a genius and exited it a forty-year-old businessman worth a hundred fifty million bucks, this househusband who watched bad TV, this profit prophet who owned five apartments in the Dakota alone and a big-ass estate out on Long Island. ~~He~~ doted on ~~his~~ son. ~~His~~ wife intercepted ~~his~~ phone calls, which is I get that sometimes we ask too much of people, because sometimes you do something too well, and one day you look up and you're all of a sudden just another phony among a world full of them. They used to say Paul was dead, except it was really the Walrus, who had died singing about peace and love, even though ~~he~~ donated bulletproof vests to the NYPD, asked us to imagine no possessions, even though ~~he~~ racked up yachts and dairy farms and country estates all over the globe. How much money did ~~he~~ give away to the poor? Ask yourself that. In what ways did ~~he~~ help any kids at all? The answers are: zero and in exactly none. Two of ~~his~~ apartments in the Dakota were used for storage alone. ~~He~~ became the self-centered bullshit ~~he~~ pretended to rail against because ~~he~~ was really railing against ~~himself~~ ... and railing against anything makes good money. Ask the Catholic church how rich it is. Ask the Dalai Lama. ~~John~~ hated himself and only *you* understood how much and only *you* knew how to help save ~~him~~ from ~~himself~~. It was up to you to compose and deliver the gift ~~he~~ craved in the form of a simple truth: tapeworm history is what you make it.

29 :::: october :::: 1969

Ry: And so you began typing the first message between those two networked computers—yours in UCLA and Bill Duvall's in the Stanford Research Institute.

Charley: Bill's system was a little easier to access than mine. The first test would be for me to log into his computer by remotely typing in the command *LOGIN*. I'm on the phone with the SRI, okay, and I type the letter *L*. I tell Bill: *Okay, I typed in the L. You get that?* And Bill is watching his monitor, and goes, *Yep, I've got the L.* So I type the *O*. He says he got the *O*. Then I type in the *G* … and there's this hesitation, and Bill goes: *Uh, wait a minute. My system just crashed. I'll call you back.*

Ry: You pronounce *L* and *O* together, and you get *Hello*—the quintessential prophetic message.

Charley: Also the first two letters of *LOL*, which may have been the more appropriate one.

Ry: (Laughter.) So Bill Duvall's computer crashed?

Charley: Bill's computer was smart. It could finish known commands. It knew the letters *L-O-G* could only stand for *LOGIN*. So it completed the command by sending the *I* and *N* at the same time as the *G*—except Bill's system only had a one-character buffer, so it experienced an overflow. That's why it went down. Bill figured that out in something like fifteen minutes. He adjusted things, and within half an hour or so everything was working great. I could type commands and use his system remotely. Our computers were holding hands.

11 :::: september :::: 2001

Doctor Dressler shook hands with Professor Johnson at the outset of each of their three preliminary sessions. He was continually impressed by her poise, cool practicality, the cognitive bite she had carried all the way into her ninth decade. It delighted him that she showed up for their meetings wearing a baggy pink sweatshirt with the words *Aging*

Disgracefully printed across the front in sparkly gold sequins. There was nothing understated about her. There was everything American. It's really quite uncomplicated, she announced, as he ushered her over to a stainless-steel chair in his office that first afternoon. I know how busy you must be, Doctor, how brief these meetings, so let me get right to the point. I'm not sad. I'm not happy. The desperate steps my country forces its citizens to take in search of a comfortable end are analogous to those which women were once asked to take in search of a safe abortion. I'll have none of it. When our pets are old and wretched, our instinct is to help them end their suffering. Why am I not entitled to the same generosity of spirit as some dumb dachshund? Doctor Dressler waited a few seconds upon her finishing, then said, reciting the first part of his script: May I ask you, Professor—are you in any discomfort? Yes, Doctor, Professor Johnson responded, the pain in the ass of having lived too long.

11 :::: march :::: 2011

—————————————————CH. 10

In college I was
a serious student
in part because
I loved learning
new things
and in part because
I never learned how
to make friends.

Not real ones,
not the sort that

didn't just say
they cared about you,
but actually
did care about you
for decades on end.

I majored in English
in addition to math.

I wanted to teach both
because for me they
formed two sides
of the same activity—
exercises in
advanced computation.

I still recall
my astonishment
the day I learned
there were Japanese words
that carried no equivalent
in English.

The idea unsettled
and enchanted me.

Komorebi:
the sunlight
that filters through
tree leaves.

Monoaware:
the awareness
of the impermanence
of all things;
a gentle sadness
at their passing.

What do people say,
if they can't say
that precisely?
How do they
think their lives?

20 :::: april :::: 1999

Only now it is us already outside the
cafeteria, which bankrupts into a riot
of dread, and on the staircase our legs
become running again, onto that second floor hall, sound objects tumbling
out—*into the classrooms, barricade the
doors, into the classrooms, barricade
the doors*—the students who in high
school know everything precipitously
becoming cognizant of all the things
they do not know.

Their faces.

You should have seen the asymmetry in their faces.

Tiny earthquakes of wreck.

First they are sixteen.

Then they are six.

They are: *Tell us what to do.*

They are: *Help us, Dave. Please.*

2 ::::: may ::::: 1945

Did you believe what you were saying?

Margot. Her name. Our wedding was last October—I remember how much I— *Christ, these goddamn hornets.*

Did you believe what you were telling Margot?

I have never believed anything more thoroughly in my life.

And do you believe it now?

Unconditionally.

Tell me why.

The Russians will be here soon, I told them. When they arrive, they will be carrying flamethrowers, grenades, and fury. Thousands of them—tens of thousands—are streaming through our streets as we speak. Their tanks— How can this— That's what I keep asking myself. Did you hear the shooting as we turned onto Schönhauser Allee? They are killing civilians for sport. Using them for target practice. There is no one left to— And the vengeance in their faces— Every look is a hundred tiny sticks of TNT about to go off. Imagine the women. The little girls. Are you sure you don't care for a cigarette, my love? No? What about you, Lieutenant?

Lieutenant Rücker took you up on your offer.

Armin. Armin Rücker.

Excellent. Armin Rücker. Armin Rücker took you up on your offer.

Good cigarettes are hard to come by, I said. It's the least we can— This isn't our world anymore, my love. We have nothing to be ashamed of. We chose to invite humanity to believe in beauty and grace. Replace the disarray of their daily lives with purpose, reverence, and security. Except the fucking degenerates lacked the evolutionary intelligence to take advantage of our grand hope.

This is important.

How could we have thought otherwise? How could we ever have believed they were capable of becoming something they weren't? Look at what we tried. A handful of years, and we reimagined Europe.

28 :::: january :::: 1986

T + .008
First of eight twenty-five-inch-long, seven-inch-wide exploding bolts fire, four at the base of each booster, freeing the *Challenger* from the launch pad.

T + .250
First continuous vertical motion recorded.

T + .678
Film developed later shows initial evidence of abnormal black smoke appearing slightly above the suspect joint in the *Challenger*'s righthand solid rocket booster.

T + 0.836
The smoke jetting in puffs of three per second, matching harmonic characteristics of the shuttle vehicle at launch.

T + 0.895
Mission Control: ... *and liftoff.*

T + 1.000
Mike Smith: *Here we go.*

T + 1.298
The *Challenger* shudders like a skyscraper in an earthquake as the main engines come up to full thrust, the astronauts receiving a massive kick in their backs.

T + 1.482
Launch Commentator: ... *liftoff of the twenty-fifth space shuttle mission ... and it has cleared the tower ...*

T + 3.501
Despite her training, Christa McAuliffe is stunned by the percussive roar across her skin.

T + 5.674
Internal pressure in the right-side booster recorded as eleven-point-eight pounds per square inch higher than normal.

T + 7.724
Shuttle starts roll over maneuver.

T + 8.000
Dick Scobee: *Houston, Challenger. Roll program.*

T + 10.000
Mission Control: *Roger roll, Challenger.*

T + 10.847
Flight Dynamics Officer: *Good roll, flight.*

T + 11.000
Mike Smith: *Go, you mother.*

T + 12.284
Behind Ron McNair's forehead it is 1959. It is the kind of hot, muggy summer day that makes it hard to breathe.

T + 14.000
Judy Resnik: *LVLH ...*

T + 14.751
Behind Ron McNair's forehead it is Lake City, South Carolina, site of the notorious lynching on February 22, 1898, that resulted in the mob murders of the city's Black postmaster and his infant daughter.

T + 15.000
Judy Resnik: *Shit hot.*

T + 18.354
Mike Smith: *Looks like we've got a lot of wind here today.*

T + 19.000
Dick Scobee: *Yeah. It's a little hard to see out my window.*

T + 21.000
Behind Ron McNair's forehead it is Ron McNair, nine years old, without forethought refusing to leave the segregated public library unless allowed to check out the armful of books he is carrying. The librarian calling the police first, then his mother. The animated *yes* suffusing him an hour later as he walks out the front doors into humid sunshine, mother by his side, relishing the acute weight of all that knowledge hugged to his chest.

T + 27.000
Mission Control: *Throttle down to ninety-four.*

T + 27.803
Flight Dynamics Officer: *Ninety-four.*

11 :::: march :::: 2011

—————————————————————CH. 11

I am thinking just now
about Coltrane, Bill Evans,
and Jimmy Cobb
sitting around with Miles
in his recording studio,
doing no more than
clowning, having a bit
of a laugh with each other.

And then, without warning,
there was *Kind of Blue*
unfolding like a blossom
made from sound.

—————————————————————CH. 12

I am thinking just now about
how it's one thing
to play jazz,
improvise over a couple
set chords,
and another thing altogether
to invent a new
musical grammar
with hardly any syntax.

Don't play what's there,
Miles used to say.
Play what's not there.

—————————————————————CH. 13

No, dear, that's not it,
my mother would say
when she couldn't say
anything else.

10 :::: june :::: 2015

My father phoned his friends back home in the evenings. A few had decided to stay behind because they were stubborn. A few to defend their houses. Others because they were too poor or sick or worn down to leave.

My father's friends told him the bombs were still falling. They told him now and then gunfire would break out in our old neighborhood.

People we had known died every day.

Schoolteachers. Storeowners. Neighbors.

Snipers picked off women as they sprinted down streets to find food in the shops with no food in them.

Sometimes it was government forces. Sometimes Daesh. Sometimes the rebels. Sometimes it was Mr. Putin, sometimes Mr. Obama.

I heard my father say: Not Fazli.

I heard him say: Not Karim, too.

Mustard gas.

Chlorine.

Sarin.

We did not know and then we did.

For months my father did not ask how I was doing. You could tell he already knew. Later he told me he thought things would get better. He told me he thought all I needed was time.

Before dawn one morning, standing side by side, packing, scent of freshly baked bread blended with his Old Spice aftershave, my father asked me: Mahmoud, do you want to leave? Is that what you want?

I want to take a boat to Greece.

Greece? What is in Greece?

In Greece there is a road you can use to walk to Berlin.

My father did not say anything. He did not look over at me. He kept packing.

Then he said: Do you know how far Greece is from Egypt? Do you know how far Germany is from Greece? You should not think these things.

I cannot go to school here.

Listen to me, Mahmoud. What lies behind us in life comes to feel like a dream after a while. What lies ahead of us comes to feel like a hope. Let me tell you something. Are you listening? Hope always cuts you. That is what hope is good for.

The other kids run after me. They call me bad names.

Hope is like a sword. People die when they hope. Those videos you watch? Europe is nothing like fancy cars. People who make the journey never come back. Even those who survive die.

I can work there. I can send you and Mama money.

What kind of work will a boy like you find in Berlin?

I will deliver bread. The government will help me. In Germany, the government helps everyone. It is not like here. And soon you, Mama, and Ana can afford to join me. We will be together again.

My father did not say anything. He did not look over at me some more.

Then he said: I know a man.

8 :::: august :::: 1974

The Father of Us whispered into our ear one night as we wandered into our dreams:

Listen to me, Sugar. We are divorcing The Mother. Everything will be different from now on.

Later—maybe hours, maybe seconds—we were awakened by capable arms swooping us up, a warm shoulder pressed against our drowsy cheek, the arranging of us among the disorientation of blankets in a cold car's back seat. Only then did it bud in our wobbly mind that it wasn't The Father of Us carrying us into brightness. It was the wreckage herself carrying us into noise. She had packed us up like a bag of dirty laundry. She had thrown us together like a toybox at the end of the day.

The Mother drove our little sister and us far away from devotion.

Next we knew, we were in some crummy motel room with mold-spore carpets the shade of crusted-up bodily fluids.

We were in Columbus, Ohio.

Des Moines, Iowa.

Denver, Colorado.

Back among the wooded hills and nutrient deficiency of Corning, New York, with new locks on the doors and a freshly installed alarm system monitoring our minute-by-minute bewilderment.

Before long everything became whose house is this?

Whose daughters?
The next courtroom.
The next dim-eyed shrink.
The next inorganic judge.
We gradually learned to love that racket and thrum.

11 :::: march :::: 2011

———————————————CH. 14

The politenesses,
the good listening skills,
the expressions of empathy,
support, trust, genuine warmth—
all those traits that made
friendship into itself:
they all felt contrived to me,
mechanical as my
awkward, angular
body does even now.

Shinrinyoku:
literally *forest bathing*:
walking deep into woods
to find replenishment.

Kintsukuroi: the art of
repairing pottery,
using gold or silver
to join the shards

in order to understand
how a piece is always
more beautiful
for having been broken.

11 :::: september :::: 2001

The little girl frozen almost directly below the red ball frozen in mid-air—stiff pigtails, pale blue dress covered with pale yellow flowers, scuffed white shoes, wildly present—has grown up in the blink of an I. Ryana can see herself running on the track team in high school, hurrying through octaves beside her piano teacher in Ganado, dashing through classes in college, gradually fathoming that nearly everyone bolts out of the same starting gate, yet almost instantaneously some begin stumbling over their shortcomings and circumstances and disinterest in living, really living, losing their traction, their will or their way, falling behind, and it hits Ryana one day as she sits in the front row of a lecture on evolution and biodiversity that she is one of those who won't stop, who will keep on sprinting through the rest of her life's glittery facts and revelations, and that prospect releases a thrill through her ribcage that just won't cease.

28 :::: january :::: 1986

T + 28.000
Mike Smith: *There's ten thousand feet and Mach-point-five.*

T + 30.000

Mission Control: *Engines beginning to throttle down, now at ninety-four percent.*

T + 33.684

It is Christa McAuliffe savoring the tug of her widening smile atop seven million pounds of thrust, a new breath every three thousand feet.

8 :::: december :::: 1980

It was the room you stayed in at the YMCA for sixteen bucks, so noisy with hacking and snoring and weeping and hammering at the walls in outrage and ecstasy that you moved to the Sheraton in midtown, where you had this hooker sent up, just like Holden in the Edmont, petite and grizzled at eighteen. You told her you would call her Sunny, even though she said her name was Anna, and you told her to call you Jim Steele, even though she knew better. You sat in the blah easy chair under the lamp in the corner and Sunny shinnied into your lap, back pressed into you, flittering her right foot up and down until you asked her to take off her dress and get into bed, but her slip, leave her slip on, you told her, which is you crawled in beside her, clothed, and talked to the ceiling, sharing all the whiteness of that moment, how the world is just this story that repeats itself, Jesus Christ Our Savior hunched over trying to stifle a giggle at the desk aswarm with turquoise butterflies, except it occurred to you Sunny's voice was all high and whiny and increasingly reminded you of a stepped-on mouse, her being a foreign language you couldn't even say hello in, so pretty soon you paid her twice her rate and told her politely to and so forth, which is why you ended up sleeping late. You looked at the digital clock on the night-stand and it said all redly 2:00 a.m. You looked again and it said all redly 10:30 a.m. And the sun was pissed off outside the floor-to-ceiling window and you shaved and showered and laid out on the bureau your talismans for the cops to find later: your miniature leather Bible, your expired passport, your snapshot of a '65 Chevy and one of you and some those refugee kids, the kids from Vietnam, plus your favorite still from *The Wizard of Oz*: Dorothy wiping away a tear from the cheek of the Cowardly Lion, an image that shredded your soul because you wanted to catch every child as he or she fell, it was why you had entered this luminous sixth plane of existence, you were certain of it, plus it felt like you were just falling yourself and would never, ever hit bottom, or what happened next was meant to be from before time. That part was easy enough to get. That part and the part about the whole thing being so much bigger than guilty or not guilty, right or wrong, five hollow-points or six, because—

20 :::: april :::: 1999

Because Dave are in the second-floor hallway, directing students away from doubt and into all that growing up, when we don't hear the human-sized crow step out of the stairwell behind us.

Don't hear the crow aiming.

That dimension where shadows are the same as furious orange ocean waves.

2 :::: may :::: 1945

This is essential to understand.

It was meant to be from before time. The Reich will go under and the Reich will rise again. Today does not represent some sort of final judgement, merely one more step in the greater war. History repeats itself until history gets history right. And so—here we are. Just the three of us. Bathed in the light of this oil lamp in this recklessly still cellar, while Berlin suffers historical vertigo. The only thing that defines our capital tonight is its memories.

Your brother-in-law saw things differently.

If you move again, Armin— Do you understand me? I'm not fucking— I— Excuse me. I don't mean to raise my voice. I didn't know how tired we were until we stepped through that door. It felt as if we had come home. Like we could rest. It strikes me— Squabbling is quite beside the point. I know we have a handful of negligible differences of opinion. Yet the truth remains we are family. And surely no one would argue that family is anything save one of nature's masterpieces. Do you understand how much I love you both? Surely there have been times—of course there have been—but you trust me to take care of things, and I will not let you dow— God*damn* it. I have to confess: I have *never* tasted a cigarette as excellent as this. There is a certain almost indefinable—what?—spiciness to it. Yet I do believe it is their lack of filters that works the magic.

28 :::: january :::: 1986

T + 36.990
Telemetry data show the shuttle's computer system responding properly to wind shear by adjusting the ship's flight path.

T + 37.000
Ron McNair, body shaking violently, two-point-five Gs of acceleration jamming him back into his seat, practices his sax solo behind his forehead.

T + 38.398
Dick Scobee confirms with himself he has bought a Valentine's Day card for his wife, Virginia June.

T + 40.000
Mike Smith: *There's Mach one.*

8 :::: august :::: 1974

And everything became The Mother howling into the phone, became why would you want to see your father after what he's done to me, became child-support dyspepsia and alimony chills and *the girls are mine, so get your goddamn fingers out of their frontal lobes.*

     It was heaven on earth.

     Only the opposite.

11 :::: september ::::: 2001

Doctor Dressler realized over the course of their first meeting how many times he had heard Professor Johnson's arguments in other mouths. Her reasoning was familiar. Her reasoning was his. Doctor Dressler is appalled at the botched suicides committed in isolation by desperate people who don't possess the expertise necessary to succeed. Most fail to grasp how difficult it is to kill oneself. Instead, they mimic maudlin movie models. They overdose on pills, ending up with wrecked livers. They jump off squat buildings, ending up with fractured pelvises. They throw themselves beneath slow-moving trains, ending up legless, armless, pointless. They blow out their brains, ending up mentally trashed, in a situation a thousand times worse than the one from which they originally wished escape. At this point in their conversation, however, Professor Johnson's argument took an unfamiliar turn. Ever-rising prices, she says, ever-mounting spoilage, ever more political instability managed by ever more authoritarian regimes, absolutely, she tells him, but also the consumption of fresh water at a rate ten times faster than the stuff is replenished in Africa, the Middle East, India, Pakistan, China, the US. The greatest mass extinction of species since the disappearance of dinosaurs sixty-five million years ago—*and* at a pace one to ten thousand times faster than average. Habitat loss. Acidifying oceans overwhelmed with plastic mites. Why in the world would I want to add to it any longer? Professor Johnson inquires.

20 ::::: april ::::: 1999

> Then everything became we don't hear the first
> guess from the crow's carbine combining with
> our thorax's design.

The second with our neck, jaw, tongue, teeth.

We barely sense it, this us all at once smashing into
blue lockers, clobbering into the tiled floor.

11 :::: march :::: 2011

—————————————————————CH. 15

That's where I—

28 :::: january :::: 1986

T + 45.000
Launch Commentator: *Engines at sixty-five percent. Three engines running normally. Three good fuel cells. Three good IPUs. Velocity twenty-two
hundred fifty-seven feet per second. Altitude four-point-three nautical
miles. Downrange distance three nautical miles.*

20 :::: april :::: 1999

That abrupt uncanny taste of ourselves.

That chewing of our own teeth bits and tongue scraps.

8 :::: december :::: 1980

Down in the hotel restaurant: southern omelet with country bacon, American cheese, hash browns, onions, sausage gravy, one glass of orange juice, three cups of black coffee—and from there off to buy a mint copy of *Catcher in the Rye*, which is you let the Prince of Peace inscribe it for you: *From Holden Caulfield to Holden Caulfield. This is my statement.* After which you returned to your room to take an alpha-male dump, reminding yourself as you hunkered on the can that some events are eternally immutable and humbling, praise be, and, as you walked out of 2730 for the last time, the mystical number of reincarnation's cycle, higher consciousness reaped, lock clacking into place behind you, the tapeworms awoke in your intestines and whispered in unison, quick as hornets teeming: *Just pack up your bag and go home, Mark. Get the doorman to call you a cab. Return to Gloria. Nothing has happened. Everything is possible. For Jesus said*—which is when The Light of Our World interrupted them in his infinite wisdom and compassion, screaming: *No one speaks for me, goddamn it, you fuckwits, for it shall begin to feel unto you like you're inhabiting a movie, but forget not that you* are the director now, *and that little pussy with the twelve-string playing hell music is just one of your actors, and you shall tell him to do anything, and he shall do it, because see how they run like pigs from a gun, see how they FLY, you sons of bitches.*

11 :::: march :::: 2011

——————————————————CH. 16

That's where I was—
in my classroom, teaching—

students Friday-afternoon fidgety,
marker raised
ready to emphasize
the same numerical point
for the umpteenth time.

I heard myself
pronouncing the words
linear functions

—and next—

—you don't really know
what happens next, do you?

You think you do,
but you don't.

10 :::: june :::: 2015

A week later my father and I were sitting across the table from a man who arranged things for a smuggler.

We were in a tiny café on the waterfront.

In the harbor bobbed a traffic jam of empty fishing boats, lime and white and blue.

The arranger was tall and skinny, his arms no thicker than mine. He talked to my father about me like I was a sack of salt propped in the corner. He was so black he was almost purple. The whites of his eyes were not white but yellow.

My father tried to haggle with him, but the arranger would have none of it.

If he does not want to go, he said, this is not a problem. Hundreds of others are waiting.

My father looked at me, back at the arranger.

What do we do? he asked.

You give me a hundred Euros. Then you go home and prepare. Pack one small knapsack. No more. I will call you. You must be ready to leave right away.

2 :::: may :::: 1945

You believed there was something splendid about the situation you three inhabited.

The intensity. The way the world had concentrated our whole lives into— This spot, I told them, is flawless. Can you sense it? Us, here, together. We have entered a variety of fairytale. Out of all the possibilities, we have located this perfect scene through which to resolve our corner of the story.

Although you weren't quite done with that story yet, were you.

It was essential for them to hear— I needed to— We fought as long as we possibly could, I told them. Longer than any other army in the world would have fought. Do you know what my final orders read?

Tell me.

My final orders read: *Fight. Hold. Breakout. Reinforcements en route. The dead impose upon us an obligation of loyalty and obedience.* I commanded my troops to keep faith, and they kept faith.

You were speaking to them in the flak tower in Humboldthain Park.

Yes.

And you told Margot and Armin—

You two have lived side by side with me through these final weeks. I love you both for it. The gratitude I— The entire time you witnessed German generosity in action. You saw us take tens of thousands into the bunker when the Soviet shelling commenced. Mothers. Children. The elderly. You heard our babies being born in the maternity ward, tomorrow coming into being all around us, even as we sealed the entrances, lowered the steel blinds, surrounded the tower with the few hundred soldiers left us. I ordered our anti-aircraft guns on the roof lowered toward the approaching Third Shock Army. Blow off the steeple of that shitass church, I commanded. Do what it takes to give me a clear line of fire. The railway cuttings will serve as a dry moat against a frontal assault.

But they didn't launch a frontal assault.

They were advancing from every direction at once, ants swarming a wounded spider.

11 :::: september :::: 2001

In the Second World War, Doctor Dressler told her over the course of their second session, reciting the next part of his script, while it dawned on him that Professor Johnson didn't sound so very American after all— she was far too mindful, self-effacing, comprehensive in her views for that—in the Second World War, Switzerland closed its borders to Jews. My country thereby forced refugees to return to their murderers. Today we have a new kind of refugee turning up at our borders, begging us to help them end their lives. How can we deny them by forcing them to return to their living deaths? Isn't that a type of murder-by-proxy as well?

20 :::: april :::: 1999

Only now it is we barely sense this swarm of hands descending, grabbing us by the arms, the scruff of our shirt, dragging us into faintly osteoporotic Doug Johnson's biology lab, our colleague with whom we have shared conversations maybe twice during our tenure here, behind the desk at the front of the room, even as we try scrambling to our feet and crumple, our reptilian brain doing most of the work by this point.

11 :::: march :::: 2011

—————————————————CH. 17

And next this squall

of dizziness
skirred over me.

The classroom
blurred out.

Surprised,
embarrassed,
I took a step back.

I recall thinking:
And now it is 2:46.
What an ordinary day
it has seemed so far.

I recall thinking:
This must be
what fainting
feels like.

8 ::::: august ::::: 1974

And yet no matter what we did we couldn't stop thinking about The
Father of Us, even for a little while.

You could see him reducing.

There were spans we weren't allowed to become a fraction of him
for weeks on end as The Mother busied herself eating her own entrails.
Gnawing, she wandered from room to room in the house that wasn't
our house, checking the viability of those new locks.

Yet, when he could, The Father of Us called covertly.

Snuggled beneath our covers at night, Ashley's sleep purr steady across the room, we murmured our devotion into our Trimline.

He called us Sugar.

Bug.

He told us he was dimming.

He urged us to be patient. Brave. He was busy diagramming even as we spoke. Make no mistake about it. He would be back for us. One day he would return and everything would be all light again.

What we have is a temporary ghost in the machine, he explained. But we will flush it out. Today it may seem like forever, but soon it will be: When was that?

8 :::: december :::: 1980

Which is you sidled back up to that dumpy dumbass with the camera and gay Hitler mustache and apologized for the way you had acted earlier, explaining you never knew who you could trust these days, could you, it's fucking psychotic, this city, which is when it—maybe four o'clock, maybe a little later, you don't—only nobody except a couple fans were hanging around the guard booth as the sun grayed out—which is when it was ~~John~~ and Yoko standing there under the gothic archway that led into whatever it led into, and ~~John~~, in this gingerbread fur-collared leather jacket, all these dried-out animals hanging around ~~his~~ neck, was talking to said dumbass, saying *Don't forget to get your book*, which is it felt like somebody had squeezed all the air out of you, everything was activated, and you strolled over and parted your lips to say something, your hand diving into your pocket in search of your gun, except your jaws jammed up, it was so assclown pathetic, and our King of Kings groaned inside you, shrugged, and lumbered out of your heart, slamming the door behind him, yet you nonetheless held out your copy of *Double Fantasy*, and ~~John~~ turned and looked at you and looked at the album and looked at you and said: *Do you want that signed?* You could feel yourself nodding, Jesus already halfway down the block, back hunched against you like a cat on the windowsill, which is out the corner of your eye you saw that dumbass raise his camera and snap a couple shots of you and ~~John~~ as ~~he~~ scrawled his fame across your record, you couldn't believe your good fortune, you and ~~him~~ sharing the same time box, what were the chances, and afterward ~~he~~ asked if there was anything else you'd like, which made you start backing away a couple steps, instinctively, like you do with snarling dogs and grandmothers, trying to say thank you in your retreat, reaching into your pocket for your stubby .38 Special, it hitting you what a curious condition thinking was, exactly like waking up one day with a French accent.

28 :::: january :::: 1986

T + 45.217
A flash at the base of the shuttle's right wing.

T + 46.000
Behind Judy Resnik's forehead it is 1966. It is Akron, Ohio. It is standing at the kitchen counter after school, tearing open her SAT letter to discover she has become the only woman in the country to have attained a flawless score that year, only one of sixteen ever to have done so. It is a joy-flower unfurling in her chest.

T + 57.000
Dick Scobee: *Throttling up.*

T + 57.395
Mike Smith: *Throttle up.*

T + 57.628
Dick Scobee: *Roger.*

T + 58.788
Tracking cameras show first evidence of an abnormal plume on the righthand solid rocket booster facing away from the shuttle.

T + 59.753
Flickering lick of flame on the side of the booster becomes continuous.

T + 60.000
Mike Smith: *Feel that mother go.*

29 :::: october :::: 1969

Ry: That miniscule gesture changed history, didn't it?

Charley: (Laughter.) Never underestimate a geek's shortsightedness. I mean, I was just this guy getting my kicks hacking on computers. Bill and I thought it was neat the packet switch worked, two computers could talk to each other like that ... but, well, they were the only two computers on the planet doing so that night.

Ry: It took a long time before anyone even started to understand the importance of what you'd accomplished.

Charley: Another ten or fifteen years before a real commercial interest in networks developed. Yeah. And it was mostly driven by the invention—in 1971, I think it was—of this killer app you may have heard of—email.

Ry and Charley: (Laughter.)

Charley: I always think if email had existed before the telephone, people would have been all like: *Forget email. Now we have this thing that allows us to actually talk to people in real time. How great is that?*

10 :::: june :::: 2015

Four days later we were eating dinner when my father's phone rang.

The arranger told him to take me in a taxi to a meeting point.

My mother began crying before my father had finished listening to the instructions. Ana was too young to understand. She cried because my mother was crying. She wrapped her arms around my mother's legs and held on.

My father and I were only a few steps from the house when the arranger called again. The trip had been canceled. The weather had changed. The sea was choppy.

We will try again soon, the arranger said.

When? my father asked.

When God is willing, he answered, laughed, and hung up.

20 :::: april :::: 1999

Which is when Dave can feel Dave begin to proliferate into that delay around him.

Into that volume.

Jim.

Mike.

Bill.

Judy.

June.

11 :::: march :::: 2011

———————————————————CH. 18

Remember where you were
when the news coverage
began scrambling into your life?

Who you might have been talking with?

Or was it some work task
you were completing,
intent, proficient, perfunctory?

None of this has happened yet,
although it will happen
in the next two or three seconds.

As you ticked through
your routine,
I stood with that marker
raised in my right hand,
readying to make
my numerical point
about variables—

—and the classroom windows
started rattling.

It felt like a heavy
truck was rumbling by
in the street below,
even though it also didn't
feel like that at all.

None of this
had happened yet,
and then everything
was vibrating—

whiteboard, pencils,
keychains, books,
water bottles, empty chairs,
our internal organs.

The walls were making
crackling sounds.

My students exchanged
alert looks, and—

2 :::: may :::: 1945

And then they were advancing from every direction at once, ants swarming a wounded spider. When their infantry couldn't gain access to the bunker, their tanks and field artillery rolled forward and began shelling at point-blank range. The idea wasn't to bog down in a fight with us. The idea was for a small contingent of their resources to contain us while the majority rushed the city center to finish off the job. The flak tower held, of course. Two-meter-thick outer walls reinforced with spiral metalwork, armored doors, six-centimeter-thick steel blinds—how could such German engineering not hold?

But the sharpshooters.

They crept onto nearby roofs. From there they opened fire on our gun crews. Many of our fighters by this stage were no more than Flak Auxiliaries—fourteen, fifteen, sixteen-year-old kids. They became our real heroes yesterday, didn't they? When one fell, another replaced him without question.

You were trying to comfort Margot.

Please, I told her. I must insist you stop crying. My mind cannot—Look at your brother. Does he seem frightened? He's *furious* at me, yes, naturally, but fright has nothing to do with it. He feels simultaneously betrayed, cornered, and beaten. It's venom you see. If Lieutenant Rücker thought he had the slightest chance, he would jump me this very second and strangle me with his own bare hands. Isn't that right, Armin? For you, I have become a symbol of everything that has gone to shit.

Armin glared at you as you spoke, his cigarette nearly finished.

The man of knowledge must be able not only to love his enemies, but also hate his friends.

Nietzsche. But Armin wasn't listening.

He was waiting for his chance.

And so you directed your comments at Margot.

The Russians are coming for us, I told her. Can you hear them? Those vibrations are their tanks.

The reinforcements you were promised never appeared.

The officers understood talk of reinforcements comprised a category of optimism. They were intent on us believing until the bitter end. I shared their collective hallucination with my men. Yet at some point, regardless, it struck me there was at last no more faith to keep. We were quite simply running out of soldiers. There was a turning point—no—I don't remember a specific incident that brought our situation into focus for me—just this creeping awareness that everything was nearly over.

11 :::: september :::: 2001

Although at first, when she found she couldn't work at her bungalow, Ryana changed tack and attempted to take advantage of the time swelling open before her. If not time to travel anymore—that was clearly behind her now—then at least time to read all the books she had always wanted to read, despite her declining eyes. There were special glasses for that. There were audio iterations. Her whole life she had wanted to tackle Joyce, meet everyone in Shakespeare's plays. She had wanted to learn to listen to music like it was supposed to be listened to—with the same care, curiosity, passion, and lush understanding that inveterate devotees bring it, not merely as the background soundtrack to one's glass of after-dinner wine. Does she have years left? It is impossible to say. Hours? If she knew, she could plan. If she could plan, she could gain some control over this evaporation. But death invariably has other ideas. To be sure, nothing is imminent. There are aches, yes, bad ones, that goes without saying, but there have been bad aches for nearly half a century now. There is the walker, but the walker is no more than a mortifying inconvenience. Rather, Ryana notices a lackadaisical dissipation on her body's part, a creeping awareness, wedged there between bed and wall, night and dawn, that life has come down to one utterly bizarre set of circumstances after another, none of which she could have dreamed of when she was that sixteen-year-old girl running on the track team. *This* is aging? And nobody thought to tell me? All the old people you used to see *out there* when you were younger, conceived of as a different species hatched in a distant solar system, have moved collectively into your muscles and bones. Ryana felt herself decelerating into this anatomy that couldn't quite stop and couldn't quite go and couldn't even— It wasn't that she hadn't accomplished something. She had. She took comfort in that. After all, she had published a number of monographs. She had delivered papers and keynotes, traveled throughout the US and Europe doing what she did best, refining the science, refuting the loonies. She had even attained what was considered in her modest academic circle some success, surely a certain degree of respect from her peers. Yet there she found herself, wedged between bed and wall, watching the red ball hanging against that pallid sky, grasping for the first time in her life it was never going to return to earth. No—it will just hang there forever, a drop of blood in a bowl of milk. That terrible *was*. And, in the middle of this thought, nighttime bleached into daybreak, daybreak into sun blaze, sun blaze into the mailman's watery voice on the stoop—his name was … what? Dave? … she was fairly sure it was Dean or Dave—asking if she needed help, if she needed him to call the police, his rapping at her front door, and she saying in the croak of some old woman she couldn't at first recognize: *Yes, please, I seem to have ambushed myself.*

11 :::: march :::: 2011

—————————————CH. 19

And then it was
this overwhelming din
blasting through the building.
It came from
everywhere at once—

bewildering, unhinging,
and I was a little girl again
back in my father's boat
riding huge ocean swells,
my land-legs gone,
my sense of up and down.

20 :::: april :::: 1999

And then it was we awoke this morning, Dave did, with our hairy bottom warming against Linda's hairless one among the covers. Like every morning, we roused not recognizing ourselves, feeling late to our own lives. We jumbled out of bed into our suburban agitation, confusing ourselves into the day.

Jack.

Donna.

Daniel.

Anna.

Ann.

Ron.

Maureen.

Twenty minutes later, Dave waved from the driveway as we opened our car door and pivoted in. Linda waved back from the front stoop, attention already tugged toward the chronic chores that lay before her. Only as we began backing out did Dave realize we and she had forgotten to kiss goodbye.

8 :::: december :::: 1980

The songs in your head were changing too fast to concentrate on and the gleaming black limousine was easing up to the curb, its door opening, ~~John~~ and Yoko sliding in, easing away, leaving you marooned on your two-foot-square island of where, listening to the sound of disease all around you, watching the limo's red brake lights merge with traffic, you recalling how every time somebody gave you a gift it ended up making you miserable, which is you released your grip on the .38 Special in your pocket and sidled up to José from Cuba to ask where they were going. José told you The Record Plant, studio down on West Forty-Fourth, where they were working on her next single, which is you thought about how outlandish it was that the last music ~~he~~ would ever make would be for somebody else, a couple of guitar licks that sounded precisely like nothing out of the ordinary, some studio musician hired for an hour or two, which is José was explaining sometimes they got home pretty late when they were out recording, you might not want to hang around, only you said it didn't matter, you really wanted to see them again, be with them again, you wouldn't have another chance.

8 :::: august :::: 1974

Except the truth was forever seemed to last forever and The Me of Us grew up in a dirty whirlwind, became a teen, a cloudburst, a freshman at the Rochester Institute of Technology majoring in mechanical engineering, a sophomore, aerospace option.

Bring on the propulsion integration.

Bring on the stress analytics.

28 :::: january :::: 1986

T + 60.430
Data radioed from the *Challenger* shows internal pressure in the right solid rocket booster begins dropping because of the rapidly increasing hole in the failed joint.

T + 60.433
70mm tracking camera closeup: An anomalous plume appears from the fitting that couples the aft end of the right rocket to the base of the external fuel tank.

T + 60.441
Behind Christa McAuliffe's forehead it is 1985. It is July. It is explain-

ing to Johnny Carson on *The Tonight Show* that everybody already knows about how kings and generals shaped history, but what about unremarkable people, like her, what about the civilians, the laypeople, the everyday Joes—how did they experience amazement?

20 :::: april :::: 1999

And next we are Alan.

We are Roy.

We are Mike.

Norm.

Anne.

Andy.

Ashley.

Rose with the fluttery soul.

Larry with a son in Tampa.

Brenda with countless burdens.

8 :::: august :::: 1974

Ashley—she fell for the calamity's tricks, letting her take her shopping, cook for her, make her bed, clean up after her, listen to her free-associate and call it intelligence, kiss her on the cheek and call it love, tuck her in, kiss her on the forehead and call it nurture, wake her, wipe her nose, rub her shoulders, kiss her hair and call it snare, baby her when she had a cold, slip an extra twenty into her jeans when she didn't need it, wring her hands over grades, over past actions and future plans, accompany her to the Christ Episcopal Church so they could pray, perform effective socialization, bake for the poor on Thanksgiving and Christmas, treat Ashley like she would never leave, never grow up, and so Ashley didn't.

10 :::: june :::: 2015

That night I could not sleep. Excitement and fear ran together inside me. When all the noise in the house went away, I slipped out of bed and roamed from room to room, the light an endless school of sardines.

I stood outside my parents' door and said goodbye to them without using my voice.

I stood outside Ana's door and felt my sister living deep inside my heart.

In the kitchen I saw the plates and glasses we ate and drank from every day as if I was seeing them for the first time. As I took in each detail, it struck me maybe I had made a mistake. Maybe my mother was right about Europe. Maybe my father. Maybe I was not ready to leave.

Why give up what you know for what you do not know? Why want? Why wish?

All the things that could go wrong with my journey swept through me.

In my worry I started to doubt I was really awake. Maybe this is what dreaming feels like when you are in the middle of one and do not know it, yet you do a little bit. I opened my eyes, not appreciating they had been shut. It was morning, the sunlight everywhere. I found myself curled up on the couch in the living room, clatter of my mother making breakfast all around me.

There was no phone call that day, or the day after.

My father told me the arranger had stolen our money and disappeared.

These people are liars, Mahmoud, he told me. They live to steal from unlucky people like us. We have done what we could. Now it is time for us to forget all this nonsense and make the best of the life God has given us. What we have is what we have. Let that be enough.

11 :::: september :::: 2001

Only after that it was their third meeting and Doctor Dressler was reciting the penultimate part of his script:

As you know, he told Professor Johnson, the Swiss supreme court has ruled people must complete the course of action by their own hand. That means we are not talking about euthanasia. No doctor can administer a lethal injection without being liable for criminal prosecution. I am therefore required by law to ask you once more: Are you fully aware of the consequences of the steps you wish to take?

Ryana looked surprised.

Are you kidding or something? she asked.

28 :::: january :::: 1986

T + 62.000

Mike Smith: *Thirty-five thousand, going through one-point-five.*

T + 64.660

The plume from the burn-through changes shape all at once, indicating the leak in the shuttle's liquid hydrogen tank is now fueling the fire.

T + 64.937

The main engine nozzles move along large arcs in an attempt to keep the shuttle on course as its flight computers try to compensate for the unbalanced thrust.

T + 65.000

Dick Scobee: *Reading four-eighty-six on mine.*

T + 65.164

Data radioed from the *Challenger* show the first evidence of the shuttle experiencing transient motion.

T + 65.524

The left wing's outboard elevon jerks.

T + 65.991
Mike Smith: *Yep, that's what I've got, too.*

T + 66.000
Mission Control: *Throttle up, three at one-oh-four. Go at throttle up.*

11 :::: march :::: 2011

—————————————————————————CH. 20

Only after that it was
acoustic tiles falling.

A computer monitor
shuddering off a table
and crashing to the floor.

A window splintering
as if shotgunned.

All at once I was lying
on my side,
the classroom canted
at an implausible angle,
the building
heaving around me.

8 ::::: august ::::: 1974

Which is when The Mother perked up and proclaimed, washing dishes while gnawing at her viscera one evening: *This can't be happening. I should never have gotten married. I should never have had you. What a crotch I am.*

But *mama* … Ashley said, all slapped up.

Okay, maybe not *you*, exactly. You're all right. I mean *her*, she said, looking over at The Me of Us leaning on the countertop.

The Mother added: What did I do to get *her* all gummed up in my life? What did I do to deserve this shitstorm car crash?

2 ::::: may ::::: 1945

And so you decided it was time to attempt a breakout.

I ordered my next in command to continue fighting until morning, then begin negotiations. The senior officers would escape the city under cover of darkness. From there they would make their way to the border and slip out of the country. Ratlines, they were calling the routes. The last passable ones from Germany to Spain, from Spain to Argentina, Chile, Paraguay, Columbia, Mexico. We would direct the counterinsurgency from abroad.

You manned the last tanks.

We had held back a handful fresh off the assembly line. Half an hour, and we pulled into the demolished night. We moved southeast quickly, using side streets whenever possible. If we could reach the southern outskirts of the capital, we—

LANCE OLSEN

But as you approached the S-Bahn station on Schönhauser Allee—

The rumble from the tanks must have given us up. The sky illuminated with hundreds of parachute flares.

The Soviets opened fire.

With everything they had. Machine guns, grenade launchers, anti-aircraft weapons. Vehicle after vehicle exploded into flames around us. It must have been twelve thirty, twelve forty-five. Do you remember, my love? I pulled you out of Lieutenant Zürth's scout car. We— What?

She couldn't remember, could she.

Who could blame her? There was so much— Everything had gone to hell. This wasn't something for women to—

And this is when time changed.

The adrenalized haze. Yes. The acceleration.

All that, and yet you were never frightened.

There was nothing heroic about what I did, I assure you. I didn't act. My reflexes acted.

You refused to stop.

Good lord, we weren't Italians. I had my orders.

You pulled Margot out of Lieutenant Zürth's scout car and—

Perhaps you recall, my love, I said to her, how Armin, a few of the staff officers, and us dashed into the ruined apartment blocks? How we clambered through one blown-out wall to the next, making our way south toward the brewery? I— What? I understand. Of course you don't. It is better that way. Memory is the mother of grief.

And the others?

My head. I can barely—

It won't be long, Erich. I promise. What happened to the others?

20 :::: april :::: 1999

All any of us wants to do, wanted to do, will ever want to do is thank them, that handswarm, for their touch, their frantic mouth output through cell phones to the dispatchers who promise the police are on their way, will be with us in fewer than ten minutes.

Who ever imagined tourniquets could feel like tenderness?

That you could drink silver light out of your hands?

The makeshift—

Carl.

Pam.

Margie.

Sebastian with doubts in Seattle.

The makeshift pillow evolved out of T-shirts
donated by the proximate students.

Bruce.

Betty.

Jenny.

The safety blankets from the first-aid closet.

Rick.

Robin.

Ernie.

Eve.

Nothing could ever feel better.

Out of nowhere, helicopter
blades thumping.

The fire alarm blaring.

A crow blundering down the
hall yelling *Happy birthday, Adolf
Hitler! Happy birthday, Adolf!*

Our hearts sound like continuous car crashes.

And next thing we are Chuck.

We are Sandy.

Jerry.

Joan.

Walt.

Melvin.

Marv.

Mitch.

Marcia with myriad midlife misgivings.

8 :::: august :::: 1974

We became a teen, a cloudburst, a freshman at the Rochester Institute of Technology, a sophomore, twenty, an occupant of our own apartment, an effervescence of confetti, more nearsighted, less young, tall as we would ever be, unspeakably sadder, and then one winter night we were chatting with The Father of Us on the phone under the covers in our dorm room when he asked apropos of nothing: You know how I said it's all going to get better someday?

You told us to be patient.

I was wrong.

You're never wrong, Daddy.

Child support.

…?

The distance from you and Ashley.

…?

It's lifting a 747 with one hand, Bug. It's carrying an earthquake on your back. We need an Adjustment Day. It's either that or a Glock 19. A SIG Sauer P320. Personally, I would prefer the Glock 19.

You've always been the best researcher.

The Glock 19 in nine-millimeter Luger is ideal for a versatile role, thanks to its reduced dimensions compared to the standard-sized option, quote, unquote.

We love you so much.

I know you do, Sugar. And now Daddy needs your help. Do you think you can help Daddy?

…?

Sugar? You there?

You hear that, Daddy?

Hear what?

That's the sound of us already on our way.

11 :::: september :::: 2001

Ryana missed bumping into her colleagues and friends in the hall on the way to her office, striking up amicable exchanges about so little, some segment they had both caught on the news, a recipe attempted, yet she missed her students more, how it seemed irrevocable that they appreciated her when working together, intuited Ryana steadily nurturing even while steadily challenging and chaperoning them into the profession. A few went on to teach and research. Most she isn't sure what happened to. Either way, the instant they left Rice a mnemonic half-life set in—that time it took for her to lose her initial impact on them. A year or two, and most had fallen away. Three, and she stopped receiving overly polite requests for recommendations couched in questions she knew she wasn't expected to answer about how she was doing. A decade, and all postcard or email traces ceased. Granted: she might still encounter one at the odd conference, but those looks they swapped—the awkward smiles in an elevator, passing each other in a busy restaurant, one trying to place the other, verify it was really who it seemed to be, despite the disquieting shape shifts—left her queasy. How can two people work together so closely and forget each other so completely? Wading into the warm dark sea, up to her thighs, her waist, her breasts, the vague recognition visits Ryana that it has quite possibly been decades since she has heard from the last one. A few cells. A few cells more. It's the strangest thing, isn't it, how her body feels as if it has become increasingly translucent, just a shadow behind a pane of frosted glass.

28 :::: january :::: 1986

T + 66.174
A luminous blob appears in the exhaust plume from the side of the righthand solid rocket motor.

T + 66.650
Data radioed from the *Challenger* show pressure in the shuttle's exter-

nal liquid hydrogen tank starts to drop, marking a massive leak.

T + 67.764

Several flame feathers on the bottom and top of the booster merge into one.

T + 68.000

Mission Control: *Engines are throttling up. Three engines now at one-hundred-four percent. Challenger, go at throttle up.*

T + 70.000

Dick Scobee: *Roger, go at throttle up.*

2 :::: may :::: 1945

What happened to the others?

I don't know. It was every man for himself. The last thing I remember before taking your hand, my love, I told her, is Lieutenant Zürth's bloody face. He stood outside the wreck of his burning car, waving a Luger—the last weapon left him. He was shooing us away as if shooing away a flock of bad dreams. *Go! Go! Go!* His voice receded behind us as we scrambled into the debris.

Fifteen minutes later you were here.

Fifteen minutes. Five days. I don't know.

10 :::: june :::: 2015

In the middle of dinner on the fifth day—I remember like it is taking place this very minute: I am raising a bite of baby eggplant stuffed with walnut and red pepper to my mouth—the arranger phoned again.

He said hurry up.

Call a cab.

28 :::: january :::: 1986

T + 70.773

CNN correspondent Tom Mintier: *So the twenty-fifth space shuttle mission is now on the way, and after more delays than NASA cares to count. This morning it looked as though they were not going to be able to launch, but—*

11 :::: march :::: 2011

—————————————CH. 21

In music,
Miles used to tell people,
silence is always
more important
than sound.

And the strange
thing now was how
nobody screamed.

Nobody said a word.

The students had never
been taught how to behave—
what expressions to wear,
how to interact,
what gestures to perform,
where to look, how,
which emotions to undergo.

Naturally we all knew
we were supposed to seek
shelter under a desk,
yet we all continued
to hover where we were,
because I think we
were convinced
what was happening
wasn't.

28 :::: january :::: 1986

T + 72.204

Data radioed from the *Challenger* show divergent up and down motions in nozzles of both solid rocket boosters.

T + 72.284

The righthand one pulls away from one of the two struts connecting its aft end to the external fuel tank.

T + 72.325

A cloud of orange fire looms higher on the other side of the main fuel tank, closer to the *Challenger*'s crew cabin, grows rapidly.

T + 72.525

Acute lateral acceleration to the right slams the shuttle with the force of .227 times normal gravity.

T + 72.730

The flight deck crew sees a silvery glare enveloping the crew cabin.

T + 73.000

Mike Smith: *Uh-oh.*

8 :::: december :::: 1980

Another way of saying this is the next six hours lasted four seconds be-cause the gleaming black limousine was already easing out from traffic and drifting up to the curb, the door already swinging open. Yoko slid out first, then ~~him~~ a few heart scrambles later, and the tapeworms … oh, man, you should have heard them … they were whisper-singing all magical … they were the Vienna Boys' Choir … the voice of someone saying she loves you for the first time … and ~~Dr. Winston O'Boogie~~ stood there looking up, admiring the pinkish nightglow over Manhat-tan, and *do it* ~~he~~ stretched wide and Yoko stepped through the black wrought-iron gate *do it* under the archway and *do it* ~~he~~ fell in a few steps behind her *do it* which another way of saying this is there has always been a big person and a little person brawling inside you, and all your life the big person has been winning, but today it felt different somehow, like this world was really some other world in which the little person could beat the big person for once, which is the ~~man~~ who would be dead in five minutes glanced at you as ~~he~~ passed, briefly took in the album ~~he~~ had signed still clutched to your chest, and you could tell ~~he~~ didn't recognize you anymore, didn't even remember talking to you just a couple hours ago, the tapeworm whisper-singing was getting louder, like the ~~man~~ who would be dead in five minutes and you were accelerating inside their song, and all these burning buildings flickering past, and so you took two or three steps toward the archway, which ~~he~~ had started to enter, and you thought—what did you think? You thought—

29 ::::: october ::::: 1969

Ry: You didn't even think about email.

Charley: Networking was designed for a small group of nerds. Even by the early 1970s there were only like fifteen computers connected through ARPANET. Think about that. The World Wide Web? Three hundred eighty websites created every minute? Seventy-eight million visitors dropping by Pornhub a day—ten million more than the entire population of the UK? No way.

Ry: Trying to imagine a computer smaller than a room.

Charley: We literally thought we were developing a mechanism to allow joint problem-solving among a handful of researchers. UC-Santa Barbara got on board. Then the School of Computing at the University of Utah. And, um—

Ry: Who could foresee the huge drop in communication costs?

Charley: The advent of the PC?

Ry: Data mining? Cloud computing?

Charley: Prescient was the opposite of what we were.

Ry: And now we're talking about what? The Internet of Things sounds so quaint, like Saran Wrap.

Charley: The idea of cheerfully giving away our privacy to maintain the illusion of friendship and popularity?

Ry: (Laughter.) Who wouldn't want to live in such a place?

11 :::: march :::: 2011

—————————————————CH. 22

Their eyes said:
Are we living inside
a video game now?
Is that where we are?

Their eyes said:
You're the teacher.
Help us.

—————————————————————CH. 23

I kept trying
to edge up
onto my knees,
only the floor kept
rolling out from under me.

—————————————————CH. 24

It struck me I should shout
something comforting,
tell them everything
would be okay,
all they had to do
was hold on tight.

Except when I
opened my mouth
my jaw snapped down
and I bit my tongue,
hard,
and next thing I—
we—

20 :::: april :::: 1999

We are floating in a gray desert that isn't a desert.
A gray weather that isn't weather.

The handswarm is talking to us again.
We fight to open our eyes.

The wallet in our back pocket, inside photos of what had once been a family, is bobbing in front of me.

Who is this, Mr. Sanders?

This is my wife Linda, we don't answer, my life-love, with her dark brown shag and confident grin announcing: *Look at where I am, where I got to on my own.*

And these, Mr. Sanders? Who are these?

Four girls in various stages of operatic puzzlement in the presence of their exasperating rents.

Multiple grandchildren looking like multiple
grandchildren look everywhere on the planet,
except none of the others are ours.

The handswarm holds each photo before us, saying:
See, Mr. Sanders—these are the people who love you.
These are the reasons you need to hang on.

We close our eyes to make them go away while we
wait for the police below this pre-hurricane sky,
but the police, rather than appearing, unravel into
a slow contemplation of vacancies and downpour.

They don't arrive in twenty minutes.

Not in forty-five.

Not one hour.

Two.

Three.

10 :::: june :::: 2015

The traffic on the way to the meeting point was heavy. We arrived fifty minutes late to find the arranger very angry with us. He looked down at my knapsack dead-faced and said it was too big.

I could not take it with me, he said.

My father apologized for the delay. He explained it wasn't our fault. It was congestion on the streets.

I was just a little boy, my father said. I needed the things I had packed to get through the journey ahead. I needed—

The arranger turned and walked away.

My father followed, begging. It was difficult to watch him give up pieces of himself like that.

When the two men returned, the arranger told us to call another cab.

On the way he asked for the smuggler's twelve hundred Euros.

As my father counted out the money, the arranger's phone rang. When he hung up, he said: We have to go back. It is not safe tonight. Too bad. But this is how it is sometimes.

20 :::: april :::: 1999

Several thousand years later, faintly osteoporotic Doug Johnson hangs a sign in the classroom window reading: 1 BLEEDING TO DEATH.

(That would be us.)

2 ::::: may ::::: 1945

Fifteen minutes later you were here.

Fifteen minutes. Five days. I don't know. Time was no longer working.

And this is where the last SS officers had entrenched themselves.

A young sweaty-faced second lieutenant welcomed us at the brewery's front gate. I told him what had occurred. I am afraid by then my pistol was pointing at the back of Lieutenant Rücker's skull. My free arm held Margot close. The officer led us through a courtyard, where civilians from the neighborhood who refused to surrender milled about in one area. In another, soldiers continued to execute deserters in an orderly fashion. At the top of a staircase the second lieutenant handed me his oil lamp, pointed down into the cellar running beneath the complex, saluted, and vanished back into the methodical turmoil.

We are catching up to the present.

We wandered the maze, searching for a quiet space of our own.

What did you see?

We passed through the makeshift military hospital, a food storage hall, passed by officers standing around a barrel in a corridor, hurriedly feeding papers into a fire, smoke hazing the air. Farther on, several men in an alcove were interrogating a bulging Russian officer. They were shouting at him. The officer's hands were tied behind his back. His chin rested on his chest. One soldier reached forward and slapped him. Hard. It was clear the poor fellow didn't understand a word of German.

It was clear it didn't matter.

And then you were here, Erich. You felt yourself entering the fairytale.

The din fell away and it was this oil lamp, this windowless room. Margot hugging her knees in the corner. Armin with my pistol aimed at him. He had finished his cigarette. I had finished mine. I offered him another. I thought it might—

We are almost where we need to be.

11 :::: march :::: 2011

—————————————————————CH. 25

The strange thing was
how none of it
would stop.

I said to myself:
Twenty seconds.

I said to myself:
A minute.

I said to myself:
*Just ride it out
a bit longer
and we'll all
get to go home.*

I closed my eyes
and counted breaths
until the tenses changed.

Only the problem
turned out to be
not that the world ended.

The problem
turned out to be
that the world
kept ending
over and over.

11 :::: september :::: 2001

While we are in a position to waive some or all costs for those in finan-
cial difficulties, Doctor Dressler spelled out, the usual breakdown is as
follows. A one-time two-hundred-franc fee for joining our organization
(here he caught himself beginning to wonder for some reason whether
he and his wife should try that new Italian restaurant just down the
street tonight—it was Tuesday, after all, their weekly dinner date, and
the restaurant came with a necklace of twinkling recommendations
by friends), followed annually by an eighty-franc membership charge.
Those wishing to commence the procedure must pay four thousand
francs upfront—without, I should emphasize, he said, any guarantee
the actual process will proceed. (A quaint bistro that could seat, at
most, twelve or fifteen, which meant he should make a reservation
sometime this morning.) The medical consultations and prescription
for the Pentobarbital will be an additional thousand francs. Should

things move forward, there is another twenty-five-hundred-franc installment to cover our expenses. (Doctor Dressler and his wife have always taken great pleasure in visiting new venues, but never quite as much as in returning to familiar ones. They tended to order the dish they most enjoyed, unable to see the upside of risking a foray into uncharted territory.) We can also organize the funeral and take care of administrative affairs, should that be something you're interested in, for an additional three thousand francs, payable in advance. Without those costs, the sum is in the neighborhood of seven thousand and seven hundred francs. With them, ten thousand seventy. That's about seven thousand eight hundred US, and ten thousand three hundred, respectively. May I ask if you have any questions or concerns at this point, Professor Johnson?

8 :::: august :::: 1974

Then he asks another question, the blanched man with the too-short red tie behind the front desk at the Corning Quality Inn, his cannula chirping oxygen: You his daughter?

We are.

I could tell, he says, a little boast in his voice. Room 243. Elevators over there.

Three minutes, and we are walking down a corridor that looks like all corridors in all Quality Inns everywhere. The carpet a geometric yawn in various shades of who cares. We feel our body becoming unable to forget it, the woozy lights lining our path, our cracked knuckles rapping on the faux wood door.

The Father of Us stands before us with his angelic grin in his bulky olive-green spacesuit parka, hood raised against the night bluster and security cameras.

Can you feel the blaze in every cell of your skin? he asks, muffled.

So much so, Daddy.

Then we're getting somewhere, Sugar. Let us share.

29 :::: october :::: 2072 :::: 10:31 a.m.

—let me just—yes—nearly thirty thousand specialists, potential investors, and influencers at other universities and in corporate headquarters and media nodes around the globe.

The breakthrough I am thrilled to tell you about today constitutes the realization of a project first conceptualized and initiated nearly a century ago. What has ensued since serves as testament to humanity's deep-seated curiosity, its practical bio-computational problem-solving ingenuity, and its social conscience. At the same time, what I am about to share with you, I should emphasize, is in its very early days—in a sense, indeed, we might say early in its very first day, its very first hours.

Let me introduce my subject to you with a number: 180 billion.

11 :::: september :::: 2001

Because Ryana missed bumping into her colleagues and friends, missed her students more, yet her husband Jerry. Her— She could never think clearly about him. When she tried, her thoughts roiled into white static. That's what happens when you love somebody and they leave you against their will and yours. She met him at a socializer in graduate school when there were still such things as socializers in graduate school. Jerry had been impersonating a student studying biology, although everyone knew he would always be a musician at heart. He played sax and told Ryana, as they uncomfortabled by a bowl of sangria in some elderly professor's house (an elderly professor who, in retrospect, Ryana appreciates, must have then been thirty years younger than she is now), that it was all about what jazz could do to the molecules in a room—you can feel them rustle and spark, you know? Every time Jerry said something like that, Ryana fell for him a tiny bit more. He was unhurried in the world, had never sprinted a day in his life, and never intended to. He was adorable. Effortless. And it wasn't long before he dropped away from the biology program altogether, formed a combo, and started playing in clubs around Houston, then Austin. He was as happy as Ryana not bringing any more fragile bodies onto this rented planet, so they settled into child-free solitude, taking satisfaction in their chosen professions, their frequent travel (Jerry almost always accompanied her on her trips to speak or do research; Ryana almost always attended his gigs), what they came to think of as their very rich hours, until one morning in their early fifties she rolled toward him to give him a little peck on the cheek before piloting toward the kitchen and their first pot of coffee, only to find Jerry staring up at the ceiling, plum lips parted, having peed himself, peed the sheets, his heart attack sweeping across their future and burning it to the ground.

11 :::: march :::: 2011

——————————————CH. 26

And then,
all at once
everything
voiceless.

8 :::: august :::: 1974

And The Me of Us is driving, The Father of Us astronauting shotgun, The One of Us reminiscing about our favorite passages from the Book of Punishments.

The Bouquet of Stones.

The Investment in Water.

The Wondrous Precipitation, wherein a crook is crowded off a cliff. The Exquisite Decollation, wherein a kidnapper's mind is separated from the other thing. The Illuminated Anatomy, wherein a richesse of holes is drilled across a rapist's torso, arms, and legs; said holes filled with oil and wick; and said wicks set alight in a lambent concert of fleshfondness.

The Book of Punishments just keeps on giving, The Me of Us notes.

All the loving possibilities, notes The Father of Us.

All God's smiles.

His hearty laughs.

His warm and bloody embraces.

20 :::: april :::: 1999

The dispatchers give the distinct impression of beige.

They obvious about stanching wounds and remaining calm, remaining quiet and keeping air passages open.

Help is on the way, they say every now and then. *Just a little more hope. Just a little more—*

But Dave are rapidly manying, and the manying unexpectedly comprehends, hanging there in dim nickel glow, that every laugh every human being has ever delivered is a warning sent from the dead.

That, every time we sneeze, it is merely the departed speaking through us, checking in to see if we are still okay, still ready to stay alive a few more steps.

That every flake of skin we shed during sleep, or magnificent lovemaking, or math class, is really a very small prayer sent back to the expired saying: *Just a moment. I'll be with you shortly.*

All in one burst, the manying comprehends these things and an endless more. That everyone's entry into the dim nickel glow is a different story. One Dave chattering around us—his name is Mary—reports it was a backwards birth; another a wild flailing amid the sensation of choking; another a sliding on a lake of ice toward an oncoming freight train whose impact is a convulsion of silence. No matter how we arrive, all are convinced that in death we will remain terrified forever because none of us knows when everything will change, or if everything will change, or if everything will ever stop changing, even though that forever may last only the sliver of a second, because that sliver will be followed by one just like it, or, more terrifying still, not followed by one just like it. And one Dave—his name is Rebecca, then Robert, then Rhonda, then Ross, then Rylie—experiences that terror as red, while another as a ceaseless piercing scream, and yet another as a flannel coat exploding into flames around her as she strolls down an empty street in Denver late one January night.

28 :::: january :::: 1986

T + 73.124
The aft dome of the liquid hydrogen tank blows out and backwards. The resulting forward acceleration blasts it up into the external fuel tank.

T + 73.191
A radiant burst inflating.

T + 73.248
Single crackling noise on air-to-ground radio.

T + 73.282
White-static dazzle erupts from the area beneath the shuttle's nose.

T + 74.130
The last radio signal from the orbiter is received. On board, the lights go out. The intercom goes dead.

T + 74.587

The external tank gives up its load of fuel, which ignites in the atmosphere in what appears to be a colossal explosion. In reality this is a precipitous burn—no shock wave, no detonation—as the tank tears apart, spilling liquid oxygen and hydrogen that form a huge combustion cloud at 46,000 feet.

(Later, some television documentaries will add the expected sound effects to this footage to make it seem more believable.)

T + 74.822
Christa McAuliffe: *Hello?*

T + 75.111
Christa McAuliffe: *Hello? Hello?*

11 :::: march :::: 2011

————————————CH. 27

10 :::: june :::: 2015

By the time we walked through our front door, my father was furious. His rage worked like burning fuel. I thought he would give up for good now, but it was the other way around.

The next afternoon he was out in search of a new arranger.

Before another week had passed, we were riding side by side in a different taxi, pulling up in front of a small mosque. From there we were given directions to an abandoned house. Inside was no furniture, no rugs, nothing save bare light bulbs and fifty or sixty men and women crowded together, waiting.

Most stood, knapsacks over their shoulders or on the floor between their legs, living in their own minds.

Some sat, leaning against the concrete walls, staring straight ahead.

I saw one man walk over to another and shake his hand in greeting. I saw a group of five or six looking down, talking among themselves. Another stared up at the ceiling, listening to somebody speaking to him on his cell phone. Three women holding babies to their chests sat in a tight circle, inspecting the blank floor. I saw a couple, a teenage boy and a teenage girl, standing very close together, backs very straight, not sharing a word. I saw another man with a bandaged cheek and bandaged hand lying on his back, arms at his sides, eyes shut. I saw mothers holding their little boys' and girls' hands tightly, preparing themselves for what came next. I saw one man the color of acacia bark arguing with another the color of lava rock in a language I could not understand, then the first pushed the second in the chest and walked away.

I saw how nobody cared anybody else was there. How each believed his journey was the only one that mattered. Each had paid a lot of money, more than he or she could afford. Everybody had worked and saved. Their families had helped, their parents, their sisters and brothers.

Nobody was there to assist anybody else.

Everybody just wanted to reach Greece.

Whatever it took, that is what it would take.

The smuggler—he looked like anyone, balding buzzcut, thick mustache, five-o'clock shadow, jelly belly, white t-shirt, torn jeans—he could be selling shoes at a stall in the souk—appeared an hour later and said it was time to go.

He stopped my father at the door, telling him he could not accompany me any farther.

My father kneeled before me and took me by the shoulders. He said he had something important to tell me. He asked me if I was listening. I parted my lips to say yes, but somebody had already steered me away from him.

I looked back and the only thing I could see was a jungle of legs.

I wanted nothing so much as to go home, for everything to be quiet again.

Yet someone was already hoisting me onto the back of a big flatbed truck. Its motor was grumbling below my feet. Billows of diesel exhaust churned up. They were packing us in like sheep. Nobody paid me any attention. Grownups jostled me back and forth in order to find their own footing.

Without warning the truck jolted forward, rattling into the dark.

11 :::: september :::: 2001

No, Professor Johnson answered. No more questions. In that case, Doctor Dressler replied, I believe there's only one more item to cover: the timing. Naturally, that's entirely up to you. When—if—you decide to move forward, simply let us know and we will set the wheels in motion. While in no way a mandate, the staff does suggest clients consider arriving at the flat during business hours. That way police formalities can take place the same day. This seems to keep the local officials in good humor.

8 ::::: august ::::: 1974

And next the Father of Us is abiding in our idling car while The Me of Us unlocks our harmony to come.

We disconnect the no-longer-new alarm system inside the front door.

Unplug the mustard Trimline fixed to the kitchen wall.

Clatter two Cokes from the fridge.

Ashley, we discover with satisfaction, is snuggled sleepily beneath a knitted blanket on the living room couch, half watching our jowly five-o'clock-shadow president saying: *Good evening.* Saying: *This is the thirty-seventh time I have spoken to you from this office, where so many decisions have been made that shaped the history of—*

Ashley says hi without looking over.

We offer her one of the Cokes and flump down beside her, asking if she's up for a game, and all at once it is nothing more than two sisters bonding over Pong on Ashley's Magnavox Odyssey intravenousing the TV set.

A tiny white square tennis ball bounces despondently across a screen the value of interstellar space. A tiny white rectangular tennis racket rises to meet and bounce it despondently back to where it came from.

How was your day, Cutie Head? The Me of Us asks, popping the tab.

28 :::: january :::: 1986

T + 75.115

Under extreme aerodynamic loads, traveling at twice the speed of sound, the *Challenger* breaks into large pieces that emerge from the billowing cloud like a spray of unexpected ideas: the main tail section with engines still burning, one wing, the forward fuselage trailing umbilical lines pulled loose from the payload bay. Electrical cables flutter behind the crew cabin as it hurls through the thinning air, still climbing.

T + 75.457

A quick, startled breath, the beginning of another, and the flow of oxygen into the seven astronauts' helmets stops.

20 :::: april :::: 1999

feel ourselves oming increas
ly isspoken. We ent an uncoor-
dination ween wind and anguage.
A stuttering of the on o ogical. An
epistemol aphasia. A   collective
mutism at   't ective

Da
D-d-d-da—
in—da.
L||||||||||||||||||||—
Lin.
Lin. Da.

Linda.

Wah—

Were— ?

Were are— ?

Where are you?

28 :::: january :::: 1986

T + 75.863

Launch Commentator (not yet realizing what has happened, eyes on the computer screen before him reeling off data rather than on the video monitor to his left): *One minute, fifteen seconds. Velocity two thousand, nine hundred feet per second. Altitude nine nautical miles. Downrange distance seven nautical miles.*

8 :::: december :::: 1980

You thought—you thought yourself into a semi-squat, that combat stance you've seen in movies, aiming, calling out quietly: *Mr. Lennon,* only ~~he~~ didn't hear you, was already fifteen feet away, or maybe ~~he~~ did hear you but didn't care, or maybe ~~he~~ was tired, or maybe ~~he~~ just had to take a piss, so you helped ~~him~~ care, calling after ~~him~~ a little louder, *Mr. Lennon … John,* and as ~~he~~ began to turn you helped ~~him~~ care even more, just like they taught you on the shooting range, because ~~Dr. Winston O'Boogie~~ had changed the world, and now you were changing ~~Dr. Winston O'Boogie.~~

28 ::::: january ::::: 1986

T + 75.877
The detached crew cabin flings out of the lower righthand corner of the rabbit-ear nebula and continues along a ballistic trajectory.

8 ::::: august ::::: 1974

Which is when the first thump upstairs clocks in, meaning The Father of Us has entered the house and smuggled himself into her room on the second floor, meaning the adjustments have commenced, amen.

11 ::::: march ::::: 2011

————————————————CH. 28

And so
I lay there quietly,
breathing,
unthinking,

returning to where
I had always been.

I looked up
at the clock.

It was 2:52.

——————————————————————CH. 29

The students
were whimpering
gently
among themselves.

There was some blood
here and there,
but not as much
as you might expect.

There were several pairs
of glasses gone askew.

A handful of students
at some point
had joined me down
on the linoleum tiles.

A few had at last
tried to crawl

under their desks,
only to have their desks
and books and supplies
tumble on top of them.

I know I should
have cared more.

I know I should
have taken charge,
tended them,
started acting
as if I fully grasped
the situation and
what to do about it.

—————————————————CH. 30

I know I should
regret not taking control,
not reassuring all those
frightened hearts.

I don't.

All I really felt
was how essential it was
for me to reach my car.

2 :::: may :::: 1945

You— What? You don't seriously believe the Ivans will forget Stalingrad, do you? I asked Armin. That they will fail to remember the two thousand kilometers lying between Moscow and Berlin? Our people will suffer their recollections for decades. Mark my words.

He didn't respond.

What could he have said?

Think of all the years we have spent together. You and I have seen so much.

Please make the hornets go away.

This only seems endless, Erich. We are almost there. Now it is two minutes ago. You are at the juncture.

These next few moments will be the most important in our lives, I told them. We must make history proud.

Armin sneered. Margot remained disconnected from her life.

I am afraid it is time to kneel, Lieutenant Rücker. Face the wall, please. Hands behind your— No, Armin. Let me explain. We are done with language. Intention has given way to action. Unfortunately, there will be no survivors. Don't embarrass yourself. And for godsakes don't embarrass your sister. Would you care for another Eckstein? Perhaps that will help settle your nerves. Allow me to—

You inadvertently lowered your pistol ever so slightly to work another ciga-rette out of your pack and—

11 :::: march :::: 2011

—————————————————————CH. 31

And so I eased to my feet,
dusted myself off
as if I'd gotten some flour
on my black dress,
readjusted my clothes
and psyche,
and hurried out the door,
down the corridor
lined with confused
chatter, down the stairs,
through the main entrance.

28 :::: january :::: 1986

T + 75.926
Because it is situated on the back of his seat, and hence impossible for him to reach by himself, and because behind him Ellison Onizuka hangs in shock, Dick Scobee's personal emergency air pack remains off.

T + 75.934
Judy Resnik leans forward to activate Mike Smith's, located on the back of his seat as well.

T + 75.989
The other crew members activate their own air packs.

T + 76.437
The nose cap of the righthand solid rocket booster separates.

T + 77.000
Driven by reflex, Mike Smith releases the lever locks to his right and begins flipping electrical system switches in an attempt to restore power to the cockpit.

8 ::::: august ::::: 1974

Ashley pays the fret above no attention. Because the game is already over. Because she has already won. Because our sister's head is resting sleepily in our lap as we massage her temples with just enough friction, just enough deployment of palms, to muffle voices on the second floor while our jowly five-o'clock-shadow president, back again behind his desk in the Oval Office, says: *As we look to the future, the first essential is to begin healing th*—

The Me of Us hovers, monitoring Ashley's respiration slomo-ing into other realms. We carefully lift her heavy blond head, ease out from under her sleep weight, tuck in the knitted blanket around her.

Find ourselves rising.

Loitering in the middle of the living room.

Taking in the musty domesticity of it all, the suspension of our own nervous system.

11 :::: september :::: 2001

Just after lunch on her birthday, in the nice little café across the street from the B&B Doctor Dressler had recommended, between one sip of Riesling and the next (she had selected the sautéed scallops in a light garlic-lemon sauce; they were delicious), Ryana decides to make the call. She returns to her room, tidies up and repacks her suitcase for no reason other than to show consideration for the maid, who has smiled at her every day of her stay as they passed each other in the corridor, takes a seat at the uncomfortable wooden desk facing the wall, and considers the cell phone in her hand. During her final days in the States, revising those final letters to everyone, she had thought about Jerry continuously. It was as if the last thirty-some-odd years had never colored themselves in. Now she startles by recalling their old telephone number, startles more by listening to it ring, hearing a stranger's voice answer and say something—some distracted teenage girl smacking gum while watching something with a laugh track on her television or laptop—and hanging up when Ryana comes to understand she has nothing to say to her. She waits a few thoughts more, then dials Doctor Dressler. Done, she navigates her walker to the front desk and asks the handsome, stiff-backed young man there to fetch a taxi, if he would be so kind.

8 :::: december :::: 1980

Because you squeezed the trigger slow and steady, and it was *BOOM! BOOM! BOOM! BOOM! BOOM!*, and four of the five shots kissed ~~him~~, and each shot knew it embodied a very special kind of love.

2 ::::: may ::::: 1945

You inadvertently lowered your pistol ever so slightly to work another cigarette out of your pack and—

—he saw his opening and sprang for me.

Did you despise him in that instant?

Not at all. I forgave him. This was a very special kind of love. I am sure I would have done precisely the same as Armin, had I been as constitutionally anemic as he.

Instead—

Instead I raised my pistol and shot him twice. In the face. He seized in mid-step and dropped. It was as if he had leapt headlong into an unmoving truth.

And you thought—what?

I thought the surprise was how unbelievably loud the discharges were in our tiny cell. I reached out the toe of my boot to investigate his body, make sure there was no more brother-in-law left in it, and, as I did so, I said something reassuring to Margot. My head all high hum, I could not hear my own words.

11 :::: march :::: 2011

————————————CH. 32

Alarms blared
in the parking lot.

I didn't become
aware of them until
I stepped into the open.

Three crushed cars
lay under a partially
caved-in wall.

The air stank of gas
from a ruptured line.

Women in white masks
scurried around a pool
rapidly forming where
a water main had burst.

Other people
squatted in place,
still unsure whether it was
safe to rise.

They were videoing
each other and
their surroundings
on their cell phones,
snapping selfies,
trying to make
this minute feel realer
than it did
by framing their panic
on teeny screens.

—————————————————————CH. 33

It wasn't until—

10 :::: june :::: 2015

It wasn't until nine o'clock that we arrived at a deserted rocky beach, clumps of seaweed and empty plastic bottles scattered everywhere.

One of the smuggler's men undid the gate at the back of the truck. Everybody scrambled down. I had to hurry or I would have been shoved off.

The second the truck was empty, it pulled away.

The smuggler told us not to talk. Not to turn on our flashlights. When he got close, you could smell the alcohol on his breath. I could not make out much in the darkness, but I could hear the water sloshing nearby. I could hear the wind.

The smuggler's men passed out life jackets to those who had paid extra for them. They gave the others a chance to reconsider. They told several of the biggest guys to fill a large inflatable raft with air.

Two hours later, we were led down to the edge of the sea in small groups.

The smuggler and his men arranged and rearranged us in the raft until we could all fit. The men sat around the edge, the women with their babies and children in the bottom.

They squeezed me in near the outboard motor, facing backwards.

Two of the smuggler's men stepped aboard last. One of them pinched the primer bulb, upped the throttle, and yanked the pull rope.

Everybody's weight shifted as we eased away from shore.

28 :::: january :::: 1986

T + 78.000
A lone drogue parachute from the righthand rocket booster nose cap materializes from the surge.

T + 78.779
Some of those in the bleachers at Cape Canaveral sense hope.

T + 79.230
Streamers of smoking debris blossom in all directions.

T + 79.528
One large unidentified piece of flaming wreckage appears from the combustion cloud and seems to tumble in slow motion toward the ocean.

T + 79.656
Those in the bleachers at Cape Canaveral who felt transitory hope feel it no longer.

T + 79.880

Behind Dick Scobee's forehead it is steel light.

T + 80.301

Two solid rocket boosters emerge and corkscrew erratically through the sky.

T + 81.000

CNN correspondent Tom Mintier: *It looks ... looks like a couple of the, uh, solid rocket boosters blew away from the side of the shuttle in an, uh, explosion ...*

T + 82.575

Silence expands on television screens across the country.

T + 82.936

One by one, the astronauts realize the crew cabin hasn't depressurized. They flip up their visors to breathe.

T + 83.000

Slender white ribbons filter down against an atmosphere saturated with dark blue.

T + 85.118

Everywhere in classrooms, students exchange alert looks, never having been introduced to the possibility of this life outcome, how to behave, which emotions to express, how to express them, their eyes saying to their teachers: *Are we living inside a video game now? Is that where we are?*

11 :::: september :::: 2001

The sadness of that second plane arcing into that second tower, it comes to Doctor Dressler as he mixes the IV solution in the sun-flooded kitchen, watching a bird—a dove? a pigeon?—perched on the wooden fence behind a pine: that plane's appearance will change everything.

29 :::: october :::: 1969

Charley: Prediction is very hard, especially when it's about the future. At UCLA we had this gigantic state-of-the-art mainframe we were really proud of. It was one of only two on Earth that had four megs of memory. *Four megs.* And it cost us four million dollars. I'm seventy now. In my twenties, how could I have imagined tiny affordable PCs you could hold in the palm of your hand that carried hundreds of times more computing power than that mainframe? So no, no one went out that night and celebrated. We just thought: There's one assignment down. What are we supposed to do next?

8 :::: august :::: 1974

We blink, considering, then open our eyes to find ourselves loitering in the middle of the upstairs bedroom, where it is a different channel altogether.

20 :::: april :::: 1999

Several years later, the handswarm
begins speaking again.

Considering, we blink, fight to keep our eyes open.

A whirl of human-sized crows are flooding
through the door into the classroom.

They wear opal glare for eyes and hornets for voices and
submachine guns for arms and ballistic shields for torsos.

Those submachine-gun arms are pointing everywhere at once.

Those hornet voices are crushing the fire alarm.

8 :::: december :::: 1980

Big chunks of ~~him~~ came out across the sidewalk and you imagined ~~he~~
would instantly collapse into a pile of ~~his~~ own reputation, yet ~~he~~ kept
walking at an unbroken pace through that archway, following Yoko,
and you kept trying to feel some sort of goodbye, each bullet not only
a kiss, but also a wave from the shore as ~~he~~ waded out into the dark sea,
it was good to have known you, ~~John~~, good to have shot you.

11 :::: march :::: 2011

————————————————CH. 33

It wasn't until
I was in my own car
that I realized
I had left my purse
with my keys
back in the classroom.

It didn't cross my mind
to return for them.

I slid out from
behind the wheel
and began walk-jogging.

I hadn't covered
three blocks
before the warning siren
sounded, gray as fear.

10 :::: june :::: 2015

Somehow this is what I had always imagined: I had always imagined
the whole trip would take only a few hours and then we would be in
Greece. But it took me that long to understand we were not yet even at
sea. What I believed was the ocean was in reality some sort of shallow
channel. This was why the water was so calm.

11 :::: march :::: 2011

————————————CH. 34

You could sense
the ground rippling
beneath you as the first
aftershocks arrived.

Many sidewalks
had buckled and
webbed with cracks,
pitched up
20 centimeters.

A chimney
had collapsed
beside a cottage.

A small store
had shifted
off its foundation.

I passed people
standing in the streets
in front of their houses,
taking in the information,
realizing how unnatural
fear and reality felt.

Everybody became

curious, present,
a believer.

It was so odd,
I remember thinking,
how in those gaps
between siren blares
bird chitter suffused
the cloudy afternoon.

11 :::: september :::: 2001

The Jade Villa, Ryana is startled to discover this sunny afternoon, lies in an industrial zone. When she first researched it, first saw the carefully cropped image on the society's website, she had pictured it perched romantically in a town high above the Rhine. In fact, shadows from a vast gray machine-components factory shroud its dark-green aluminum siding. Across a narrow street, beyond a stand of gnarled pine trees: a drab soccer field. There are no sidewalks in this part of the city. The street is empty. The air smells like wet rust. Why does it matter what the air smells like? Ryana pays the chubby driver, ashy beard, ashy hair, scarred face still youthful, thanks him, wonders if he has any idea where he has just delivered her, what this moment in her life means. She gingerly makes her way with the aid of her walker across a patch of gravel, over the little wooden bridge spanning a goldfish pond, a small grassy patch on one side, a stand of pussy willows on the other. As she approaches the villa, the glass doors swing open. A skinny woman in a tidy white short-sleeve nurse's uniform steps out and welcomes her. Doctor Dressler's form floats behind her. I'm Anna, Professor Johnson, says the nurse. Here. Let me help you.

2 :::: may :::: 1945

And so you turned toward her to see if she was—

I turned toward her to find her vomiting. She was on her hands and knees, vomiting and weeping. Simultaneously. The sounds—my hearing little by little returning—the sounds she produced were quite extraordinary. They comprised the painful noises of a human coming apart. The contents of her stomach splashed onto the cement floor. Splashed again.

You wanted very much to ask her something.

I wanted very much to ask if she recalled our first meeting. We stood before a punch bowl at a military dance. I wanted very much to ask if she recalled how her nerves knew I had tumbled into love with her the second we began to speak. Her beauty. Her motherly intellect. The instantaneous and deep interest she took in my words, no matter how pedestrian they may have sounded to others. There was something chemical in our exchange. It felt as if— How to say it? It felt as if our bodies had known for ages what our minds were just then finding out.

But you didn't ask her.

There was no time. Shouts had already broken out in the hallway. Soldiers were rushing to their posts.

The Soviet tanks had arrived at the front gates.

Yes. What could never have happened was happening.

28 :::: january :::: 1986

T + 86.000

The crew cabin continues to climb, although the tracking cameras, obsessed with the bloated heart of flame, fail to capture its ascent.

T + 89.000

Mission Control: *Flight, GC, we've had negative contact. Loss of downlink.*

T + 91.299

Eyes shut, Dick Scobee comprehends what could never have happened is happening. He sees what the end of his story will look like, feels himself giving over to it, knowing at a certain point everyone becomes the same age. He wills himself present for the astounding sensations to come.

T + 93.000

The order is issued to initiate search and recovery forces.

T + 95.392

And now it is this swirl and lift in Christa McAuliffe's stomach that might mean rapid ascent or descent. Without contextual markers, which direction she is going is impossible to tell. Her body juddering through wave after wave of aerodynamic stresses, she strains to find the tiny porthole across the mid-deck to her left, just beyond the edge of her helmet, on the far side of Greg Jarvis and Ron McNair, but can't bring it into view.

T + 101.000

The altitude of the crew compartment peaks at 65,000 feet before starting its two-minute-and-forty-five-second plunge toward the ocean.

T + 101.759

Inside Mike Smith's brain, something breaks.

8 :::: august :::: 1974

The Me of Us is compelled by the shimmering yes in which we stand.

The queen-size bed has been evulsed from the wall, the wooden desk chair beside it capsized, the sheets torn back around her, the quilt jumbled on the carpet, the pillows broadcast across the room like a spray of unexpected ideas.

Her mayhem hair hide-and-seeks her face.

Her frumpy blue floral nightgown has garbled up to her armpits, revealing a pair of soiled matching underwear of the kind that encourages one to look elsewhere.

Still in his spacesuit parka, The Father of Us straddles The Was in a way that nearly obstructs our view of the pink towel stuffed in her mouth, the thin yellow nylon rope cinched around her neck.

The Me of Us notes with interest her hands and feet are still quivering, paws of a dreaming Labradoodle.

We approach the bed and take a seat on its edge.

Reach over and squeeze her jittering left forefinger—to wish her a good expedition, easy travel to other planets—but her hand flinches and yanks away.

8 :::: december :::: 1980

Which is after that you commenced hearing the sixties and seventies quietly coming apart around you and Yoko's voice screaming *John's been shot!* and José was all of a sudden blundering at you. You didn't move. Why would you move? A few eons later he reached your time-space orb and knocked the gun out of your hand, kicked it across the pavement. *Do you know what you just did?* he was shouting. *Do you know what you just did?* He seemed confused. I just shot ~~John Lennon~~, you said, trying to help him parse the relevant developments, which is it was all at once very warm—what sort of December was this?—so you removed your hat, removed your coat, put your hands atop your head, and commenced pacing back and forth under the archway. Only that didn't work. So you decided to take a seat on the curb and wait for the next part of your legend to occur, signed copy of *Double Fantasy* still clutched to your chest, mint copy of *Catcher in the Rye* still napping in the pocket of your coat bunched on the sidewalk. You passed the nothing-nowhere watching José remove ~~John's~~ glasses, cover ~~John~~ with his own jacket, Yoko caught in the God Swirl.

10 :::: june :::: 2015

Every once in a while the propeller stuck in weeds. The outboard motor clunked to a stop.

The smuggler's men seated on either side of it reached into the black water to free the blades from the tangle, restarted the motor, and we pushed on.

Nobody spoke.

We were looking everywhere at once, taking in every detail, telling stories to ourselves about what we were in the middle of living.

From time to time a baby began to cry. You could hear its mother murmuring comfort to it. You could hear the baby slowly quieting down. You could hear another baby start up in its place.

You could hear somebody cough, somebody clear his throat.

Otherwise, the night was steady wind.

The chugging of the motor.

Each of us carried only one or two bottles of water in our knapsacks. There was no room for more. I saw the sun hammering down on us by noon the next day. I saw the long trek from Greece to Berlin and felt how my feet would ache after only hours. The road would come to feel like the roads you watch in cartoons, the same background slipping by you over and over.

I made myself remember the schlager music.

The full supermarket shelves.

We were wedged in so tight, it was dangerous to shift. When someone tried to stand and stretch, others would shout at them to sit down, sit down, what do you think you are doing?

People elbowed me without thinking.

A big man used my Converse All Stars as the floor of the raft to keep his own hiking boots dry. When I pulled my feet out from under him, he waited a minute and then rested his boots on mine again, until the tops of my feet throbbed and went numb.

Eventually I took off my sneakers and socks and held them in my hands because I had promised my mother I would take care of my things.

There was nowhere to go to the bathroom.

I do not know why, but I did not think about this before we left.

Soon the stink of pee rose from us.

At the spot where the channel emptied into the Mediterranean, the waves swelled.

The raft began to pitch. I reached down to tighten my life jacket. It was then I felt the crinkling inside, figured out the smugglers had stuffed empty life jackets with newspaper instead of foam to get a little more money out of us.

8 :::: august :::: 1974

It's then that the galaxy stops, just for an instant, just for a caught breath, and The Me of Us can sense The Was has entered the God Swirl. The perception is so beautiful, bathes the room in such tinseling wonder and serenity, we could—

Can you help me out here, Sugar? The Father of Us asks over his shoulder. Do you think you can do that?

11 :::: september :::: 2001

Helped by Doctor Dressler, Anna ushers Ryana into a clean, open, neutral room. In the far corner, a double bed on wheels with a yellow and red spread beneath a window overlooking that cluster of gnarled pines. Beside the bed, an IV stand, a wooden chair, a black metal side table on which sits a black CD player, a stack of discs, a box of tissues. At the foot of the bed, two more wooden chairs with another black metal table between them. On that table, another box of tissues and a black digital clock with numbers the color of the potted fern beside it. Above the chairs, a large oil painting of a small red farmhouse among green hills under an overcast sky that suggests more English than Swiss countryside. Near the glass doors, a large off-white sofa. You could almost believe, Ryana considers as the nurse guides her, one hand gripping her elbow, one her wrist, walker abandoned outside— you could almost believe you were entering some holiday rental at a ski resort. The former owners, Doctor Dressler explains as he assists Anna in lowering Ryana onto the bed, adjusting the pillows behind her, getting her comfortable under the knitted blanket, had the constellation of Orion embedded in tiny halogen lights across the ceiling.

What a choice, he says. Anna asks if Ryana would like the vanilla ice cream she requested in advance. That would be very nice, Ryana replies, taking in those strange bright pinpoints, Doctor Dressler's thick graywhite outburst of hair, this moment, and this one, struck by the thought: *How curious—all these things are occurring around me one last time, just like they do around all the others propped in this very bed several times a week.*

11 :::: march :::: 2011

————————————————CH. 35

My parents' house
stood near the harbor.

Because of rubble
in the streets,
the groups of people
gathered everywhere,
everything occurring
at once, it took me
longer than usual
to reach it.

The front door
was locked.
I banged with my fist,
calling out their names,
but no one answered.

I found a rock
large enough
to smash a pane of glass,
reached in,
undid the catch.

20 :::: april :::: 1999

And then *Hands on heads, hands on heads,* the hornet voices whirring.

Follow us out NOW.

(Another voice offers staying with all the Daves.)

EVERYONE OUT

GO

GO

GO

(They can carry us, the other voice offers.)

(Only they can't carry us.)

(They can improvise a stretcher.)

(Only they can't.)

11 :::: march :::: 2011

—————————————CH. 36

I discovered my parents
upstairs in their bedroom.

They had cached themselves
beneath the covers
in their nightshirts,
waiting for facts to arrive.

My mother smiled at me
with her bad teeth.

My father squinted,
confused by all this
newness going
on around him.

I told them
we had to leave.

They told me they
had to get dressed first.

I told them
we didn't have time.

10 :::: june :::: 2015

And then a bright white pinpoint began blinking far off to our right.

The raft eased around and piloted for it.

The light belonged to a motorboat that would take the smuggler and his men back to shore.

The motorboat neared until it bumped into our raft. The smuggler scrambled over us and aboard. His men followed. He yelled back at us to choose somebody to drive. It was not hard, he said. The crossing was up to us now. Several days, and we would be in Europe. Good luck. May God be with you.

As the motorboat pulled away, we could hear him and his men laughing.

28 :::: january :::: 1986

T + 110.250
Range safety control officers send radio signals to detonate the self-destruct package on the right solid booster rocket.

T + 110.252
Range safety control officers send radio signals to detonate the self-destruct package on the left solid booster rocket.

T + 112.492
CNN correspondent Tom Mintier: *We're awaiting word ... they're ... they're holding their ... I'm sure everyone is. In the center of the fire and the smoke, you can't see any form of ... and, uh ...*

8 :::: august :::: 1974

The Me of Us opens the bedroom door like The Father of Us asked and walks into the jowly voice below saying: *When I first took the oath of office as president five and a half years ago—* Only inside us, it sounds as if he is saying something else. Inside us, it sounds as if he is saying: *If only I could escape this pileup, this shattering life. If only I—*

29 :::: october :::: 1969

Ry: And so you had no clue you were going to be famous one day.

Charley: Famous? (Laughter.) I didn't become famous. About fifteen years ago, I had *Hollywood Squares* on one morning in the background while working. Out of the blue I hear Tom Bergeron going: *What was the first thing sent on the Internet?* The answer, needless to say, was our LO of LOGIN. And I remember how it hit me: *Will you look at that? I've become a trivia question!*

28 ::::: january ::::: 1986

T + 113.022
The astronauts on the flight deck see the Atlantic Ocean roll into view as the crew cabin stabilizes nose-down.

29 ::::: october ::::: 2072 ::::: 10:33 a.m.

And so let me introduce my subject to you with a number: 180 billion.

Why is that a quintessentially significant one?

Because that's the estimate of how many people have died before us over the course of human history.

28 ::::: january ::::: 1986

T + 114.000
Cameras pan across the crowded bleachers at Cape Canaveral: the faces of the nearly five hundred baffled spectators—including eighteen school-children visiting from Christa McAuliffe's hometown of Concord, New Hampshire—some exchanging aimless language, some grimacing

into sunshine, some gaping up, trying to take in the information from above as it hits them how unnatural fear and reality feel, how everybody all at once wants to become a believer.

11 :::: march :::: 2011

——————————————————CH. 37

Age had made
my father denser,
heavier, unwieldy,
my mother airier,
less cluttered,
as if most of her
had already gone
on ahead.

They progressed
methodically, each
movement a difficult
equation.

I gripped my mother
by the elbow,
helped her down
to the ground floor,
then dashed back up
for my father.

11 :::: september :::: 2001

While Anna slips into the kitchen, Doctor Dressler presents Professor Johnson with two final forms to sign—the first confirming the professor's executor (a far-flung nephew whom she hasn't seen in decades), the second her wish to be cremated. Anna reappears with a smile as they wind up, bright red bowl in her cupped hands.

28 :::: january :::: 1986

T + 115.000
CNN correspondent Tom Mintier: …

T + 116.000
CNN correspondent Tom Mintier: …

T + 117.000
CNN correspondent Tom Mintier: …

2 :::: may :::: 1945

And so it was already happening.

I crossed to where Margot was dry-heaving and kneeled beside her. I reached out my free hand and began rubbing her back, massaging her horrors. Her body continued to undo itself. She had retreated into her own choked closet. There was no room for me in there.

How did that make you feel?

I understood. I had seen this many times before.

You loved her deeply.

Until we met, I was merely a series of misconceptions.

You wanted to express that love. By rubbing her back, you wanted to let her know you were there for her.

I wanted to let her know that, ever since we met, she had never been alone. She would not be alone now. I wanted to let her know with my palm that everything would be all right. I would take care of her.

And as you rubbed her back—

And as I rubbed her back, I brought my pistol up to her temple and fired. Her body jolted as if receiving an enormous electric shock, then flinched into itself.

11 :::: march :::: 2011

————————————CH. 38

We were in
the living room,
baby-stepping toward
the front door,
when the tsunami arrived.

10 :::: june :::: 2015

Next the night became chaos.

People called back and forth in fright. We did not know how to operate the motor. We did not know how to steer properly. We did not know where we were going or what we were supposed to do or even if we had enough gas to reach our destination.

In the end, an Algerian teenager volunteered. It became clear right away he had never driven a boat before. When he took the grip, our raft began speeding around in circles, creating more waves among the waves.

Everyone panicked.

Some called out that they wanted to go back, this was crazy, there was no way we could continue like this. Others argued they had paid too much, risked too much, to stop now.

This is how we will die, somebody said as if asking for a haircut.

Prayers rose up into the darkness.

(It was then I understood people remember God only when they are in trouble.)

The Algerian stared grimly ahead.

He would not give up the grip. He pushed others away who tried to reach for it. He knew what he was doing, he shouted when they tried to reach for it. Give him a chance. He would show us.

11 :::: september :::: 2001

Doctor Dressler talks Ryana through the concluding steps while she spoons up her dessert, luxuriating in each sweet cold vanilla mouthful. Next, he reaches over and slips in the CD she had asked for at their third meeting—Miles Davis's *Kind of Blue*, fifth track: "Flamenco

Sketches"—less melody than slow, forlorn sonic shades blending one into the next.

It was always Jerry's favorite.

28 :::: january :::: 1986

T + 119.995

Mike Smith's vision blurs. His thoughts smear into his seventeenth year, a dentist's chair, the removal of his wisdom teeth. The oral surgeon tells him to begin counting backward from one hundred by threes. Nitrous oxide seeps through his attention. Voices—whose?—recede as if the chair he is occupying were rolling away down the hall, out the front doors, across the vacant street beyond.

T + 120.003

Ninety-seven, Mike Smith mouths.

T + 122.000

Today, at this altitude and cant, the Atlantic Ocean appears to be pale green with sepia traces.

T + 123.565

Behind Ellison Onizuka's forehead it is 1952 again. It is not Lorna Leiko Yoshida, the sharp, assertive fellow student he met, fell in staggering love with, and married while completing his studies at the University of Colorado. It is neither of his daughters, Janelle or Darien. It is just the no-light strewn with diamond-dust stars suspended in the middle of his reeling mind like an always.

T + 123.797
Mike Smith mouths: *Ninety-four* ...

T + 124.489
Eyes wide open, Dick Scobee is flying down the Pacific Coast Highway on a motorcycle at a hundred five miles per hour, a hundred ten, sunset oranges and yellows flicking off his faceplate.

T + 126.790
Christa McAuliffe is crying.

T + 128.000
Mission Control: *We have no downlink.*

T + 129.103
What Greg Jarvis doesn't know, wouldn't care anymore if he did, is that it will take search ships using sonar more than a month to discover his remains and those of the other six in the crumpled cabin that will have come to rest on the ocean floor one hundred feet down and about twenty-five miles northeast of Cape Canaveral. Greg Jarvis's body will be located in the lower mid-deck along with Ron McNair's and Christa McAuliffe's. During salvage operations to raise it, his will accidentally become dislodged and float free of the wreckage, disappearing into the murky waters. On April 15, the last day scheduled for recovery, it will once again be spotted, bobbing just below the surface, and returned to shore. His wife Marcia will henceforth refer to this event as a miracle.

T + 136.102
Behind Ron McNair's forehead it is Ron McNair floating weightless three hundred miles above sea level, sans shuttle, sans spacesuit. He

wears nothing but a flowery Hawaiian shirt and oversized shorts. He is playing his sax better than he ever has in his life while peering down at the blue and white globe that fills three-fourths of his view. Maybe that's Europe, he speculates. Maybe it's the Middle East. So what? He can sense every question mattering a little less, then a little less than that.

T + 142.696
Blood continues diffusing through Mike Smith's cortex as he uncouples from the world.

T + 143.119
Crying, Christa McAuliffe struggles to tell whether her eyes are open or shut, whether she is awake or something else.

T + 148.330
The acrid reek of the high-energy ion vibrations, dying stars, is ubiquitous—the same reek astronauts report clinging to their spacesuits upon reentry to the shuttle from extravehicular activity: a mixture of welding fumes and brake pads.

T + 155.307
The motorcycle on which Dick Scobee is flying down the Pacific Coast Highway fluxes into the oblate spherical steel ball at the end of the fifty-foot arm on a G-force centrifuge trainer pivoting faster and faster around its huge chamber. He has the impression his teeth are being sucked out the back of his head. His vision narrows. The familiar blinders close in. His smile widens. Come on, he thinks. Let it strange.

T + 158.519
The crew cabin reaches a terminal velocity of 207 miles per hour.

T + 159.302
Judy Resnik tries to will herself to lose consciousness.

T + 165.881
Judy Resnik fails.

11 :::: september :::: 2001

Ryana hears a click and looks over.

10 :::: june :::: 2015

It took a very long time, but he was right: at last the Algerian got control of the raft and people started to settle down.

We were in open waters. Everything looked the same in every direction. The waves grew bigger. Sometimes they became so high it felt like our raft was rising to the top of a hill before smashing back into the sea below.

Sometimes the motor cut off and the Algerian had to restart it.

Above, the only light was the black khimar of sky sprinkled with glitter. I tried to fall asleep and hours smeared into more hours and next a blockish old woman was pointing.

We made it, she was shouting. *We made it.*

20 :::: april :::: 1999

Two crows stay behind to wait with us until a
paramedic arrives.

One of them reaches out its claw to check my chest for respiration.

It's okay now, the crow says. *You made it.*

We raise a hand and rest it over the
claw because we find sometimes a
claw is enough.

And somewhere else other crows
lead students and teachers out
the classroom door.

We wave goodbye,
even though we don't
wave goodbye.

We smile at them, even though we can't.

11 :::: september :::: 2001

Ryana hears a click and looks over. The nurse has begun videoing. She steps forward and commences setting up the IV drip. Everything feels to Ryana as if she just woke up and can't figure out how she got here. She closes her eyes to better focus on the music emerging around and through her. A few seconds, and Doctor Dressler lets her know he is starting the saline solution. A few more, and she can feel him place the IV valve into her palm, fold her fingers around it. I know we've been through all this before, Professor Johnson, Doctor Dressler says, and I apologize for the repetition, but it's the law. At this point I must ask you several questions to verify your mental competence. Would you please tell me your name, date of birth, where you are from, and why you are here. Ryana answers each question carefully. She wants to make sure to get everything right. And do you know what will happen when you open the valve? asks Doctor Dressler. Yes, Ryana answers, a little taken aback. Of course I do. And do you want to die? asks Doctor Dressler. Yes, Ryana replies. I want to die now. Thank you, Doctor Dressler. I appreciate all you've done. Thank *you*, Professor Johnson. If you would like to die, you may open the valve when you're ready.

11 :::: march :::: 2011

———————————————————CH. 39

The door exploded
off its hinges and—

20 ::::: april ::::: 1999

And we find ourselves watching the students from an impossible vantage point, some outlandish security camera angle, even though that doesn't happen, and we see them single-file down the hall, the staircase.

In the commons, they slosh through three inches of water showered from anxious sprinklers.

Pizza slices bobbing.

Knapsacks jellyfishing.

The fire alarm cuts off.

The stillness replacing it is the loudest sound we have never heard.

A crow holds open the front doors. Stops each student for the count of two. Taps him or her on the shoulder.

Says: *Sprint.*

Says: *Run for your life.*

11 :::: march :::: 2011

—and a wall
of seawater
rushed us.

I reached out
for my parents.

Himari, my father said,
and then the living room
was churning with chairs,
a couch, planks of wood,
pillows, newspapers, shingles,
a toaster oven,
a bright red gas tank.

We held hands
momentarily,
but the waves
tore us apart.

I heard my mother screaming
she couldn't breathe
as I scrabbled
onto the counter.

The water rose
to my neck in seconds,
rushed into my mouth.
I had to tilt back my head
to catch gulps of air.

I recall thinking:
This is how I will die.

Of all the ludicrous possibilities,
this is how death will find me.

28 :::: january :::: 1986

T + 174.020

Dick Scobee dreams about parallel universes, his mind moving at two hundred seventy miles an hour, the speed of flustered human thought. From his perspective, the dream lasts hours and hours. He sees how in most of the universes there will never have been a *Challenger*, a Cape Canaveral, an America, any lifeform on this planet other than the bacteria transported here on space dust four billion years ago. In a few, NASA will decide to scrub the launch. In one, despite a partial O-ring burn through—something that has happened before on numerous missions—the flight will be a success, the astronauts return safely to earth, and all but Christa McAuliffe's name will be immediately forgotten, relegated to prosaic space program annals, the public having long ago tired of the relentless monotony of that whole underwhelming enterprise. It is in this universe that Greg's celebrity status will bleach out in less than a week, that he and Marcia will welcome their daughter into the world on October 29, 1988. They will name her Nicole and topple instantaneously into frenetic love with her 26,000,000,000 cells. Twenty-four years later, Nicole will slide woozily into the backseat of an Uber across town from her apartment in Ithaca, New York, at the end of her second year in Cornell's MFA program. Befuddled by the effects of a whiteblue pill imprinted with the word *SPACE* slipped into her palm by a fellow student with a cleanly outlined stubble beard and man bun in the midst of a rowdy, wine-soaked party inhabited by thirty people performing the Bohemian Writer's Life for each other and themselves, Nicole will slide woozily into the backseat of that Uber, never to be seen again. Her last perception will be that the seat on which she is sitting, the windows all around her, the gearshift, the air conditioner, the floor mats are exuding Leonard Cohen songs in a language she doesn't know. *Oh, man,* she will think. *Oh, man, oh, man.*

29 :::: october :::: 1969

Ry: *Man.* Look at this. How did our time together shoot by so quickly? I'm afraid we only have a minute or two left, Charley. To wrap up, let me throw you a curve ball, if that's okay with you.

Charley: Sure.

Ry: Would you tell us a little about what kind of kid you were? Would we have been able to recognize in him the guy sitting across from me today?

Charley: When I was seven or eight, I wished for two miracles. First, I wanted to own a library that housed every book ever written. Second, I wanted a magic carpet that would carry me anywhere in the galaxy I wanted to go. Thanks to the Internet, I've pretty much got both those now.

10 :::: june :::: 2015

And next a blockish old woman was pointing.
We made it, she was shouting. *We made it.*

We looked where she was looking and saw lights on the horizon.

I could not believe my eyes.

The Algerian swung the raft around. The more we studied them, the more we understood the lights could not be part of a coastline. They were moving like we were moving. They changed course when we changed course and now they were approaching us.

The lights of a Greek island turned into the lights of a large fast-moving boat.

One of the European rescue patrols must have spotted us.

Just like that, we knew we were going to be all right. From here we would be escorted to a registration center. There they would process us. This would take some time. Everybody said with the Europeans you needed to be patient. They were slow, but good-hearted. They would feed us. They would give us beds and a place to shower. Before long I would be in Berlin.

When the boat was maybe a hundred meters away, its floodlights blazed on. The night burst into a blinding white fog. That is when the machine gun on the boat's bow opened fire. Bullets splattered into the water in front of us.

A young woman with a pretty face shrieked. Others joined her. What was going on? What were they doing to us?

The Algerian threw the motor into reverse, but the large boat kept coming.

8 :::: august :::: 1974

Because The Father of Us grabs her right wrist with both hands and yanks what's left out of bed.

Because The Was lands in a bulky clump on the carpet.

Because The Me of Us joins in, grabbing her left wrist.

One, says The Father of Us.

(We shut our eyes tight.)

Two, says The Me of Us.

(We shut our eyes tighter.)

Three, says The One of Us.

And with that we wrench-drag The Was across the room, through the doorway, and onto the landing, where The Father of Us re-secures one end of the yellow nylon rope around her neck, the other around the banister, and over goes the past.

28 :::: january :::: 1986

T + 186.401

The first chunks of debris begin splashing down into the Atlantic. The junk rain will continue for the better part of an hour, preventing search forces from entering the zone, which will cover an area of 486 nautical miles. In the end, the operation will include twenty-two ships, six submarines, and thirty-three aircraft. To discourage scavengers, NASA utilizes the codename *Target 67* to refer to the crew cabin and *Tom O'Malley* to refer to the human remains.

11 :::: march :::: 2011

———————————————CH. 40

The strange thing was
how I recall thinking:

> *Thank you:*
> *everything can only*
> *get better*
> *from here on out.*
>
> Standing there on
> the countertop,
> palms braced
> against the ceiling,
> taking in those
> little gulps of air,
> my goal became
> nothing more
> than to get through
> the next five seconds,
> and then the next five,
> and then the five after those.

8 :::: august :::: 1974

Below, something snaps.

28 :::: january :::: 1986

T + 189.339

What had been slow blood seepage through Mike Smith's brain now bursts into lavish flood. He sees sapphire phosphorescence. He thinks: *Thank you.* Sees his wife Jane give him The Look when he shows up late again for a parent-teacher conference. Thinks: *Thank you*. Sees his children Scott, Alison, and Erin frozen in mid-run, mid-game, in the backyard one summer morning. Thinks: *Thank you*. Sees the hover of a shiny lime-green tennis ball caught in a late-afternoon orange-and-yellow strobe during the best game he has ever played. And then he sees nothing at all.

8 :::: august :::: 1974

Below, something bumps against the wall.

10 :::: june :::: 2015

I want to tell you: I was not afraid when the shooting began. I would tell you if I was, but I was not.

I could not understand why anyone was screaming anymore.

People only scream when they have hope.

11 :::: september :::: 2001

With her thumb, Ryana flicks open the valve. She hears Doctor Dressler shift out of the chair. He kneels by her bedside, takes hold of her IV arm with one hand and squeezes gently, gently begins stroking her forehead with the other.

11 :::: march :::: 2011

———————————————————CH. 41

I'm sure by then,
no matter what you
had been doing,
no matter with whom
you had been speaking,
you were fixated
on the real-time coverage
rushing at you,
somewhere inside of which,
just out of sight,
I was trying to live.

28 :::: january :::: 1986

T + 197.546

All at once Judy Resnik can no longer call up why, after her parents divorced when she was a teenager, she prepared and filed a court case so her custody could be switched from her mother to her father. Can no longer summon why she divorced a kind, bright, thoughtful man named Michael eleven years ago. All that comes to mind is the brief glimpse of her mother breaking into a reflexive grin one morning as she sleepily shuffled into the kitchen when she was eight. How Michael and she touched foreheads, leaned into each other, held that pose for ten, maybe fifteen seconds, their special form of kiss. Her soft, unnamed resentment at Michael's ability to take her unhappiness away.

10 :::: june :::: 2015

What is remarkable is how people act when they know they have no choice about how to act—that vacant-faced recognition, like someone has reached inside and switched off their souls.

The Algerian cut our motor.

You could sense the idea rippling through us all that somehow we must have drifted back toward the mainland. We must have been spotted by an Egyptian military patrol.

The boat swung alongside us.

Giant white waves rolled against our raft.

I thought we were going to capsize. I got ready to hold my breath. I told myself I must swim away from the others fast as I could when the raft went over. Otherwise, they would pull me down with them.

11 :::: march :::: 2011

—————————————CH. 42

From here on out,
you know very well
what happens, don't you.

28 :::: january :::: 1986

T + 201.884

From here on out, it is nothing but green with sepia traces cramming the flight deck's windows. The horizon has pivoted out of view, the coast, any sense of depth or perspective.

29 :::: october :::: 1969

Segue Music: 10 seconds: Chorus of "Magic Carpet Ride" by Steppenwolf, fading in and out …

Ry: I'm Ry Himari, and you've been listening to Random Access Memory. I hope you enjoyed the trip. Next week we'll be dropping back to 1971 to visit with George M. Martin, retired biogerontologist at the University of Washington, who first proposed that information within a brain could be copied or transferred to digital storage, thereby reducing or eliminating what he called The Mortality Risk. Please drop on by if you can.

Music Closing: Chorus of "House of Memories" by Panic! At the Disco, fading in …

Ry: And, until then, don't forget:

Baby we built this house
On memories …
And when your fantasies
Become your legacy
Promise me a place …

Music Closing: Chorus of "House of Memories" by Panic! At the Disco, fading out …

10 :::: june :::: 2015

Our raft filled with water. Several passengers dropped over the side into the sea. Straightaway they began flailing. They did not know how to swim. They did not realize how strong the waves could be. One man slid under our raft and bobbed up again three meters away, his mouth open like he was howling, but no noise came out. Many pushed their way to the back, where I sat, causing our raft to dip below the waterline and flood even faster.

I clung to the outboard motor with all my strength.

8 :::: august :::: 1974

What is remarkable is how long it takes to taxi The Father of Us back to his hotel, where in the parking lot he slides behind the wheel of his own car and vanishes into his impending.

How long it takes to drive back to the whose-house-is-this, reconnect the no-longer-new alarm system, plug back in the Trimline, turn off the TV, gently massage Ashley awake, say, mussing her mussed hair: Get your coat on, Cutie Head.

What time is it? she asks, fuzzy.

It's time for a sleepover. My place. Pizza and Coke. On me. Monopoly till dawn.

Dibs on first roll.

Done.

Won't Mom miss us?

I left her a note.

Then it's a race, our sister says, blooming off the couch, and look who's winning.

10 :::: june :::: 2015

A net dropped down the side of the patrol boat. A sailor with a bull-horn boomed orders at us. *Climb in an orderly fashion,* he said. *Do what we are telling you and you will be all right.*

11 :::: march :::: 2011

———————————————————CH. 43

The linked catastrophes
like a neural network firing:
those disabled
emergency generators
serving the reactors.

The hydrogen-air explosions.

The term *caesium-137*
entering everyday usage,
the term *exclusion zone.*

The photo of that starving dog
still chained on someone's deck.

That perfectly intact red and white
Coca-Cola vending machine
tilting alone in tall grass
in front of a trashed gas station.

28 ::::: january ::::: 1986

T + 215.730

Dick Scobee begins to experience his final breaths as if he were living in a version of one of Zeno's paradoxes. Before the *Challenger* can advance from its present position to the ocean's surface, it must reach a point halfway between the two. Before it can reach a point halfway between the two, it must reach a point halfway between its current position and the halfway point. Before it can reach that quarter point, it must reach a point halfway between the halfway and the halfway to the halfway. And so on, forever. The final arrival never arrives. Dick Scobee's final breaths last an eternity.

2 ::::: may ::::: 1945

And now we are now.

Almost. Yes. In a few seconds we will be the same age. I—

10 ::::: june ::::: 2015

At the dock in Abu Qir a group of soldiers was waiting for us. The Algerian recounted our story to the sergeant in charge. The sergeant listened with a face so loose you would have thought he was asleep even though his eyes were open just a little bit. When the Algerian was done, the sergeant explained to us that all we had succeeded in doing was to stray out to sea thirty kilometers, turn in wider and wider loops, and eventually make our way about forty kilometers down the coast.

You paid a lot of money to go nowhere, the sergeant told us. I hope you enjoyed the ride.

11 :::: march :::: 2011

—————————————————————————CH. 44

But you don't need me
to tell you any of that.

I'm sure you're near
the end of your
commute, reading
more quickly
than you should be
so you can finish
before the train
pulls into your stop.

28 :::: january :::: 1986

T + 229.303
Those still conscious on the flight deck make out waves flittering across
the ocean's surface, flock of a thousand white ibises.

10 :::: june :::: 2015

In the parking area beyond the dock, another flatbed truck idling. Another long ride through the darkness.

The world felt ripped up.

The world felt strewn on the ground behind us.

I stood pressed against the back gate. I asked those around me where the soldiers were taking us, but nobody answered.

As the truck rattled down the highway, the skyline of Alexandria, minarets the color of sand, rose up before us in the dawn. People bounced and swayed around me, even though nobody was there. You could see it in their faces. Everyone was somewhere else.

I realized I was no longer holding my sneakers and socks.

2 ::::: may ::::: 1945

And now we are now.

Almost. Yes. In a few seconds we will be the same age. I reached out and took her right hand in mine. I set about relishing my last four or five breaths, the sheer amazement of them, the touch of her touch, how we liked to note how our fingers meshed perfectly. I reflected on how good it was to have a death that did not feel important.

Was that your last thought?

No. There was one more, Erich.

11 ::::: september ::::: 2001

With her thumb, Ryana flicks open the valve. Doctor Dressler kneels by her bedside, takes hold of her IV arm with one hand and begins stroking her forehead with the other. With her thumb, Ryana flicks open the valve and

and that red ball appears

suspended in midair

those beautiful children below frozen in midgame   mid-run   how
there was love for you once   how there was

the pale-blue sheet stopped in mid-flutter

and there is that bright morning   sorting wash   fingers
finding the foil condom packet in his jeans pocket

how you lift your head to look out the window

family of shockingly white socks on the clothesline

white boxers   white panties   white brassieres   handkerchiefs

wading farther and farther into
the warm dark sea

[saying   trying to say   *your hand feels*
so good Jerry   don't ever let go ...]

you believing you would behave one way   condom
tweezed between your fingers   only to find yourself
behaving another

up to your tummy   up to your breasts

your neck

sometimes you forgive people simply
because you still need them in your life

and in a single inhalation   you fell out of love   and then
back in love again   more deeply than ever

because you never stopped sorting that
wash even as you continued looking
out the

what kind of bird

your mouth loosening

seawater trickling in

just a little longer

another breath   please

sunshine white static overrunning you

and the sound of colors   who could have believed   their exquisite

    each child elated   or secretly sorrowful   or

or

listen

they are singing across
the yard

[*may I have a cuddle now Jerry*   *may I have a*   ]

oh

11 :::: march :::: 2011

————————————————————CH. 45

Another way of saying this:
I could have been somebody else.

I could have been anybody else.

You are always part of the story
without being part of the story.

You have already lost
your parents, too,
even though perhaps
they are still alive.

This is how the present works:
we are all features of tales
we will never be features of.

At this point,
the tale is nobody's.

At this point,
everybody's.

At this point,
catastrophe keeps us
together.

20 :::: april :::: 1999

And, waiting for the paramedic, we are reminded of B films.

Where did they go?

What in the world ever became of them?

We are reminded of B films and B films
remind us of the vagus nerve.

How holding hands stimulates it.

How stimulating it lowers blood pressure and
heart rate.

How lowering blood pressure
and heart rate eases the em-
braced into relaxation and a
sense of well-being.

Because B films were by far the best films for holding
hands, and holding hands is the real reason all movies
exist in the first place, isn't it?

10 :::: june :::: 2015

They hustled twenty of us men out of the truck, step on it, along a cinderblock corridor lined with barred doors, into an airless cell built for
six people. There was one small window very high up. There were three
bunk beds. There was a hole in the floor for a toilet. Around the hole,
brown and black splatters. The stench was terrible. Next to the hole, a
single faucet. Beneath, no sink. The crush of bodies wedged me into a
back corner. I scrunched there, hugged my knees and knapsack to my
chest. You could not stretch out because of all the people. Men lay on
the bunk beds, on the floor, their legs across each other's bellies, across
each other's thighs and ankles. Some shouted to get off, only there was
nowhere to go. I shut my eyes. There was too much noise and motion.
Too much had happened in too short a time. It felt like I was falling
forever. I was so sad, worn, and then I was back in the raft, only this
time the patrol boat swung alongside and giant white waves hit us and
next I was thrashing underwater. The patrol boat's floodlight formed
a huge white egg above me. No matter what I did, the egg would not
come any closer. My chest seared. I thought: *This is how I will die. Out
of all the possible stories, this is the one about how my death will find me.*
Hands grabbed at my legs, trying to climb me like a ladder. I kicked at
them to make them go away, but they kept yanking me down. I could
not hold my breath any longer. I knew in the next second I would give
up and I knew there was nothing I could do and with that I jerked
awake because somebody in the cell had snatched my knapsack out
of my grip. I could not tell who. Everybody was sitting or standing or
lying where they had been when I closed my eyes. Some were talking
among themselves. Most were trying to sleep. I called out. I said somebody had robbed me. I said somebody had stolen my knapsack. Everybody pretended to be deaf. This is when everything became a froth of
black butterflies inside me and I started to cry. Once I began, I could

not stop. The more I cried, the more I had to cry. A hand reached out of the crowd in my direction. I believed it was reaching out to comfort me. I extended mine to take it—but it swiped my hand aside and slapped me hard across the top of my head. *Shut up*, the voice attached to the hand bellowed. *Shut the fuck up and be a man.*

28 :::: january :::: 1986

T + 231.938

Christa McAuliffe is back in her classroom, teaching. One by one, her students raise their faces to the ceiling as if the scream of jet engines all around them comes from above. One by one, their skin begins to smoke. One by one, they shiver into shafts of flame.

10 :::: june :::: 2015

For five days they fed us one meal each morning. Sometimes lentils with tiny pebbles still mixed in. Sometimes unwashed, unsifted rice. Once just four slices of bread. The heat of our bodies made the cell hotter, the air wetter. If one of us got up to go to the bathroom, somebody else would take his spot on the floor and he would have nowhere to sit when he returned. He would have to remain like that until somebody else got up. People pushed me out of the way to clear more room for themselves. A fat old man snored so loudly it seemed he was choking. A fight broke out, although I could not tell why. The man the color of acacia bark pushed the other man the color of lava rock. He stumbled over the men behind him and fell backward. His head cracked against the wall as he went down.

Later, he sat turned inward for a long time, cupping the back of his skull, staring straight ahead.

When my knapsack found its way back to me again, there was nothing inside it.

Then, on the afternoon of the fifth day, our cell door swung open and a guard shouted at us: *Hurry up, out, out, out, get moving.*

A group of policemen hustled us up the same cinderblock corridor lined with barred doors that we had been hustled down before.

All at once we were outside, crossing a dusty courtyard, the sun brash as the floodlights on the patrol boat.

We squinted.

We shuffled and tripped and kept going.

On the far side, another metal door, another cinderblock corridor, another courtyard, another metal door … and there was my father, standing before me.

I want to tell you something: If I have been a good human being, if I have done what I was supposed to have done in this life, when I die I will get to live in that moment endlessly.

20 :::: april :::: 1999

—was the remedy was the hope was the hornets was the guesses was the delay was the not was the this was the that was the mistake was the comfort was the impediment was the hope was the crow was the carbine was the beauty was the car was the driveway was the rush was the hallway was the Tuesday was the alarm was the stairs was the hazy was the solace was the numb was the lockers was the slam was the tiles was the slam was the waves was the crows was the us was the them was the forest was the desert was the gray was the not was the voyage was the not was the could was the opal was the numb was the wasn't was the kindness was the wave was the Linda was the voyage was the knapsacks was the bright was the Linda was the kindness was the teeth-shards was the claw was the hope was the Linda was the tongue was the numb was the claw was the stillness was the hope was the Linda was the peace was the hope was the gray was the bright was the hope was the sprint was the hope was the claw was the hope was the hope was the hhh—was the hhhhh—the hhhhhh—the hhhhhhhh-hh—

2 ::::: may ::::: 1945

Was that your last thought?

No. There was one more, Erich.

Tell me.

I recall realizing, bringing my pistol up under my chin, resting its hot tip just above my Adam's apple, shutting my eyes, easing down the trigger—I recall realizing there is nothing, nothing whatsoever, that brings you into the present quite like letting go of someone else's hand.

11 :::: march :::: 2011

—————————————CH. 46

Soon I found myself
teaching the same students
in a different drab building
in a different drab town
the same equations
I always teach them.

After work on Fridays
I found myself returning
to my new apartment,
listening to Miles Davis
on my couch over a beer
and bowl of ramen,
pleasantly brain dead,
pretending this is how I
want to live the life
I am pretending to live.

10 :::: june :::: 2015

And next my father swept me up in his arms. His grainy beard was
home. His Old Spice. I did not so much listen to what he was whispering to me as relish living inside the vibrations of his voice.

My mother and Ana stood on the far side of the main gates, the
happiness in my mother's face beyond saying.

All I wished to do was cut off my memories from the rest of me.

It did not used to be so hard for this world to imagine its future.

Several months later, packing bread early one morning beside me, my father raised his head and said such a thing is impossible now. He had not been talking. Now he was.

Listen, Mahmoud, he said without looking over. Are you listening? They explain to us how soon the sea will swamp coastlines like the patrol boat swamped your raft. Every day will become its own season and fish invisible even to themselves. It will be like an American movie, only true.

My father stopped talking and went back to packing.

A minute later he raised his head again and asked: How were we born into this? What did we do that was so dreadful?

I wanted to have an answer for him, yet all I could do is think about how maybe someday my family will have a nicer house in a better place than it does now.

Or it will not.

Maybe bombs will begin to fall out of the sky, bridges burn, buildings turn into tall flowers of soot once more, and nobody will ever again have a place to call *here*.

Maybe someday nobody will be welcome anywhere they travel and everybody will have to keep moving from one country to another, unwanted by everybody they meet.

Maybe trying to imagine the future is like drifting far out at sea in a crowded raft.

At night.

With no lights in view.

With an outboard motor no one knows how to operate.

Moving in wider and wider circles.

All the while facing backwards.

8 :::: august :::: 1974

Maybe what is remarkable is all the stuff we thought we knew but didn't know, but did, but didn't, as Ashley and The Me of Us sped through the darkness of the darkness on our way to our apartment that night. We became twenty all over again, a paradise of connection, a boil of confetti, and then, early next evening, a vulnerable wide-eyed sophomore listening to some detective on the phone reciting the love story The One of Us had written, and there we were performing shock, performing breakdown and oblivion, sob-asking: *You're saying my mom killed herself?* and somewhere the some detective was answering: *I'm so sorry, honey. Can you tell us anything that might help us understand what happened?* and we heard ourselves saying: *I stopped by last night and found her freaking out at Ashley. She'd been late for dinner. So I tried to defend her, which pretty soon Mom and I were in the middle of this big fight. Ashley and I took off to my place. She slept over to let my mom cool down, only— Sometimes she got like that, my mom. Sometimes she said things she didn't mean. It was just who she was. She did it so much Ashley and I even invented a name for it—AGM: Attention Getting Mechanisms. But we never— How could— I don't— How did— It was Ashley who found her?* and somewhere the some detective was asking if she and her partner could come by to see how we were doing, maybe ask us another question or two, it wouldn't take long, she didn't want to trouble us, she understood how difficult this must be for us, how inconceivable and relentless, and there we were saying: *Oh, yes, please—it would be really good to talk to somebody right now,* and somewhere the some detective was saying her partner and she would be there within half an hour, if that was okay with us—because it all felt like this thing ending, not this thing beginning, not this you're-only-getting-started thing, as Ashley and The Me of Us plunged through the darkness of the darkness into The Not Now and The Not Then, because we hadn't thought beyond that inevitable phone call as the splintering stars flicked across our windshield, all those radioactive ice chips from outer space flying in, like the future had become hammer on glass, like the sky had broken, like who could explain all the stuff we didn't know, but did, but didn't, as we eased our foot down on the gas and the everything became an illumination of bird wings through which we plunged, and we inhaled and we held our breath and we thought: *Don't give us hope, goddamn it, don't even think about it, not now,* and our car went faster and faster and we became smaller and smaller and all we could hear was tomorrow charging in, and behind that, distantly, my sister's crazy laugh, as if she might even be enjoying herself, as if she wasn't just so scared there was nothing else for her to do.

11 :::: march :::: 2011

—————————————————————CH. 47

But that's just how
stories work:
every one of them
ending in a spill
of white space.

The strange thing
isn't that.

The strange thing is
how once upon a time
we believed deeply
Hiroshima could only

be visited upon us
from the outside
by awful intensities.

Or maybe how
I didn't really know,
not in any way that matters,
that every meeting is
the origin of a leaving.

How once upon a time
I didn't even know
what a story was.

I thought I did,
but I was wrong,
just like you are now.

I didn't know stories are
the events that only happen
to other people.

When they happen to you,
they're called the world.

8 :::: december :::: 1980

Because later it will be that balding doctor holding the blown-apart
man's heart in his hands. It will be Gloria traveling five thousand miles
to the single-wide trailer they will provide you in Upstate New York,

far away from cameras and guards, where for forty-four hours at a stretch they will let you two pray together and order pizza together and forgive together and watch *Wheel of Fortune* together and enjoy the complexities of your cellular structures while listening to the screams of children falling. Only then it was something else. Only then it was just you sitting alone on the curb on a too-warm night, people keeping their distance, watching you as you thought about how this afternoon you were milling around in front of the Dakota after talking with José from Cuba, zoning, and all of a sudden out of the crowd stepped Sean with his nanny on one side and bodyguard on the other. He was five, and his face said he didn't know yet what falling meant, didn't have a fucking clue, and, as those three walked by you, maybe returning from a stroll through Central Park, you found yourself stepping forward, coming up from behind the nanny, reaching around, and taking Sean's hand in yours. He squinted up into your eyes and this electric breeze scrambled through you and you couldn't help it, *He's such a beautiful little boy, isn't he?* you told the nanny, which is when the bodyguard made a gesture like he would undo the scrambling breeze in a biceps flex if you weren't quick about it, so that's when you let go, because it was okay, everything was okay, and you smiled, stood up, took two steps back, surprised once more how hard it is to explain to other people how there is something so real about holding a little kid's hand, allowing the body to say so much by doing so little.

28 :::: january :::: 1986

T + 236.550
Christa McAuliffe reaches out and pats air to her left, searching, locates what she is looking for, clasps Greg's glove in her own.

T + 236.981

Greg Jarvis thinks: *Marcia, my love … thank you …*

T + 237.079

Here it comes, the burning children whisper into Christa McAuliffe's burning mouth. *Here it comes, the future, and it will always look exactly like this:*

29 :::: october :::: 2072 :::: 10:30 a.m.

I'm delighted to welcome you this morning—my morning, at least—to the Mind Emulation Studies Department at Cairo University. My name is Riyana Arafa. I'm a computer neurologist and chair of our program. How pleased I am to see my hologram reaching—let me just—yes—nearly thirty thousand specialists, potential investors, and influencers at other universities and in corporate headquarters and media nodes around the globe.

The breakthrough I am thrilled to tell you about today constitutes the realization of a project first conceptualized and initiated nearly a century ago. What has ensued since serves as testament to humanity's deep-seated curiosity, its practical bio-computational problem-solving ingenuity, and its social conscience. At the same time, what I am about to share with you, I should emphasize, is in its very early days—in a sense, indeed, we might say early in its very first day, its very first hours.

Let me introduce my subject to you with a number: 180 billion.

Why is that a quintessentially significant one?

Because that's the estimate of how many people have died before us over the course of human history.

180 billion.

Consider that for a moment …

Until today every person who has ever lived has disappeared from this world forever.

Most have been forgotten immediately.

A few have been lucky enough to survive a generation or two in this or that family's vague and increasingly fallible recollections.

A tiny handful of truly transformative imaginations—among them the likes of Shakespeare, Bach, Picasso, Darwin, Einstein, Saliba—survive longer through the distorting lens of their work. Yet even these names will be consigned to void if The Great Catastrophe continues to intensify as predicted and the alarming proliferation of totalitarian regimes to which we see country after country succumbing these days reaches us here in the NorAf-Euro Union.

Those regimes' existence evinces the social response to the civil upheavals we have witnessed as water, food, meaningful capital, and other resources become ever scarcer. We long ago crossed the point of no return concerning the confluence of climate change, resource depletion, and overpopulation.

Even if in some quixotic universe we could one day ameliorate, if not fully alleviate, the current situation, there would still come a time in the extreme future when our Sun itself would take the Earth with it as it enters its own fiery death throes, thereby erasing every vestige of every mind that has ever carried an idea.

Let me briefly offer up several more numbers for you. During the Roman Empire, the average life expectancy at birth was twenty-five years. By the Middle Ages, that figure had increased to thirty-three. In the late nineteenth century it began to rise dramatically due to the advent of germ theory and overall better medical care. This allowed more people to survive infancy, the most dangerous fraction of their lives. By the early 1900s the average had reached fifty-five, and by the end of the last century many adults in advanced economies enjoyed a relatively high quality and quantity of existence as the result of antibiotics, chemotherapy, and drugs for chronic disorders.

With these advances a larger problem revealed itself: despite this progress, we could never discover a way to turn back the underlying biological process of aging. The simple fact remains, the molecules that create us accrue accelerating damage. Our DNA goes through millions of ruinous events every day. As we grow older, the body's machinery designed to fix those injuries becomes ever less efficient.

Add to that ambient toxins; the diminution and contamination of our natural systems; the recurrent outbreaks of information sickness; the increase in zoonotic pandemics; and the rapid multiplication and intensification of wars to secure fresh water supplies, arable land, gas, and other fuels—and, well, it is little wonder that life expectancy has been on a steep decline for the past four decades.

Even in the best scenarios, at some point everything in the human body will go wrong in a riotous cascade. Despite our most fervent efforts, we must eventually bow to our surroundings and to the years.

The real hope for our species lies not in trying to extend our life spans. Our minds and bodies seem to have an absolute upper limit to longevity, a terminal identity, at around 115, with rare exceptions reaching the record of 122—yet never beyond.

In the end the house will always win.

Must that be the inevitable outcome? Must the narrative of each of our lives end in hush?

We have another option, and it is that I want to tell you about today.

Let me suggest, by way of introduction, that for the last century we have been asking ourselves the wrong questions, and thereby arriving at the wrong answers.

What if I were to tell you that you could keep your dead loved ones living on beside you eternally, even as you could live on beside them for as long as you wished? What if it were within your capacity to upend Wallace Stevens' philosophical cliché about death being the mother of beauty, and instead assert a different truth: that how long we live really *does* matter? That living as long as we, rather than time, decides—gathering ever more knowledge, ever more wisdom, contributing ever more to our species' development scientifically, aesthetically, socially, existentially, while each day learning to appreciate the act of living ever more fully—is infinitely better than dying before we feel done?

What if Tesla and Hawking could have lived another three hundred years? What discoveries might they have made?

Lincoln and Marx?

Buddha and da Vinci?

What if we admitted to ourselves that the awareness of inescapable death teaches us absolutely nothing about being alive except that everything we have accomplished, everyone we have ever loved, every pleasure and every anguish we have ever experienced has been and will be for exactly nothing?

When I was six or seven, my biggest dream was to be an astronaut and work on our moon base, possibly make one of those one-way journeys to our outpost on Mars, or perhaps even be among the first team to travel beyond our planetary system.

At this time I stumbled across a science fiction novel called *Skin Elegies* that made a tremendous impression on me. Its protagonists were put into therapeutic hibernation on a thousand-year flight into the heart of our galaxy. They remained roughly the same age as the day they boarded their ship.

I recall wondering how I could become as timeless as those astronauts.

Only better.

And that, in a sense, is why we have gathered here this morning.

•

What I want to tell you about goes by a number of names—Whole Brain Emulation, Encephalic Propagation, Mind Upload—but whatever we choose to call it, its attainment represents nothing less than an arrival at a bona fide singularity.

Along with a number of other neurotechnologies centers across the planet that form our consortium—I want to particularly thank Tunis University, the Libyan International Medical University, the Free University of Berlin, and Uppsala University—in 2035 we here at Cairo University picked up where the BRAIN Initiative left off following the suspension of the Constitution and establishment of the Reformation Government in the former United States. Announced in 2013 by the Obama administration, the BRAIN Initiative—short for Brain Research through Advancing Innovative Neurotechnologies—was a collaborative, public-private research undertaking whose goal was to create a dynamic understanding of our brain's function.

We soon came to realize that our objective was not to undo aging or repair an environment already spoiled past the point of rehabilitation, but instead to bypass the problems of growing old, of The Great Catastrophe altogether, in order to produce a life-extension model based on a completely different set of assumptions and means.

First, we aimed to use cutting-edge science to continue unlocking the secrets of the human brain. Second, we aimed to use those findings to upload a human mind—the product of the human brain—to a separate, longer-lasting container: a quantum computer.

When a person loses a leg or arm, hearing or vision, the sense of touch or taste, when she or he suffers a traumatic spinal injury that results in quadriplegia, we continue to imagine that person as theirself—as who they were, in essence, before the loss. When, on the other hand, a person loses to dementia their ability to contemplate, or receives a traumatic head injury that casts them into a vegetative state, we feel we have lost that individual—that that person is no longer who they used to be in any meaningful sense.

In the former cases, it would strike us as abhorrent to propose we end their life simply because a person is not inhabiting a fully functional body. In the latter, however, our society has deemed it appropriate in some circumstances to terminate life support.

Why?

Because in the latter scenarios we intuit the individual has become something other than what we conceive of as a human being—a complex identity complexly responsive to its environment.

We can lose our bodies and conceptually remain ourselves.

Take our brains away, though, and it is another matter entirely.

An organ incapable of feeling pain—weighing in at just over three pounds; comprised of seventy-three percent water; filled with nearly 100,000 miles of blood vessels; generating on average about 50,000 thoughts a day—the human brain represents a miraculous piece of natural bioengineering.

And now another number for you: 86 billion.

That is how many neurons make up an average brain. In early pregnancy, those neurons develop at a rate of 250,000 per minute. Each is connected to about 10,000 others. Together, they form roughly 100 trillion connections. Every idea we have, every sensation, every emotion, every so-called out-of-body experience, every unfolding of love, of insight, of judgment, of trust, of grief, of disgust, of bigotry, of hate, of hope, of panic, of paranoia, of lust, of humiliation, of ecstasy, of doubt, of transcendence, of intuition, of freewill, of spiritual enlightenment, as well as every neurological and psychiatric disorder from Parkinson's disease to autism, depression to schizophrenia, is a function of those neurons firing or not.

Still, how in specific terms the brain generates mind has remained a mystery until recently. The challenge of moving from the physical substrate of cells connected inside our squishy pinkish-gray organ to our mental world—our speculations, our recollections, our senses— has remained almost impossibly enormous.

Our consortium, I am pleased to announce, has met that challenge.

Every aspect of our conscious and unconscious awareness is an emergent consequence of the operations carried out by the machinery of our neurons, which can be thought of as tiny processors that know nothing except that incoming excitation or inhibition changes their membrane potential. At some threshold they respond with an electric discharge.

Put another way, the brain operates on a series of zeros and ones. The orchestration of billions of neurons is the information processor that plays the concert we refer to as our experience of being.

Once able to map the legion of operations within the connectome—the connections of all the neurons in a brain, our symphony of selfhood—we can copy a particular brain to a computer. To scan that brain, we needed to develop a 3D resolution of a few nanometers. We discovered that process by necessity destroys the biological organ as the scan moves through it, measuring and charting its computational features. The result is what we refer to as Destructive Upload. The DU produces a simulation of the entire brain in software.

Run that software, and we meet a digital mind indistinguishable from its material predecessor.

•

The software mind displays precisely the traits we view as the essence of our species—language, rationality, recollections, learning, personality, humor, bliss, sadness, and so on.

Yet within a very short period after an initial Mind Upload—perhaps hours, perhaps seconds, surely within a few weeks, months, or years—the emerging consciousness will begin to modify itself into something far less humanlike. It will evolve beyond any reasonable definition of *homo sapiens*, develop new traits altogether, and hence evolve into what we surely must call a new species—one that can as an upshot of its digital embodiment think, feel, and calculate incomprehensibly faster, more nimbly, more complexly, and perhaps in incomprehensibly different ways and to different ends than those of us not uploaded.

This new species' instinct will likely be in part to connect with—perhaps even independently generate—others of its kind: its own friends, society, pastimes—an instinct that will, it is fair to guess, lead to a networked, multi-order pan-consciousness in a brief span.

Perhaps it will even want to create its own fully imagined worlds—computer games, as it were, to keep itself amused—in which the inhabitants would not know they were no more than so much code, but rather thought and felt just like human beings. Perhaps these sub-entities will form a third-order universe, and in that universe they might create a fourth-order one in which the inhabitants did not know *they* were code, and so on.

As the Swedish philosopher Nick Bostrom pointed out nearly seventy years ago, we—those of us currently invested in the belief that we live on Earth—could in fact be those beings. There is no way to prove otherwise, no way to disprove we are even now populating a computer simulation without knowing that's what we are doing, possibly even as the original multi-order pan-consciousness entertains itself on an interstellar space expedition.

•

Through our own doing, we will thus have made it possible to transcend ourselves, engineer *homo evolutis*—the first species that directly and deliberately steers its own evolution and that of all others ... including, needless to say, us.

If we are not careful, *we* will have changed into something else as well—a species that has created its own masters and will henceforth function for no reason other than to serve them by tending their mainframes, providing them with energy, sustaining their infrastructure.

After all, why else would *homo evolutis* keep the likes of us or any other species around except to make sure the engine of their existence is kept, as it were, well-oiled and humming along?

I presume at this point some of you—as well as those protestors who have gathered outside our consortium's institutions and in several major NorAf-Euro Union capitals—might want to argue that, in light of what I have said on the subject so far, the whole idea of Mind Upload is terribly wrong from the start.

After all, it feels in some fundamental way to be against nature, a version of Icarus' flight and fall translated into cybernetic terms. *Homo sapiens* has no principled reason to bring *homo evolutis* into existence. Living forever is tantamount to being trapped inside one's freedom.

I understand these sentiments, even as I disagree with them.

My counterargument runs something like this. First, simply because a phenomenon is natural does not mean it is moral or acceptable. We fight cancer, viruses, and cruelty every day, even though they are innate facets of our existences. Furthermore, we have modified—denaturalized—our neural networks since the appearance of our species through everything from alcohol, meditation, and religious trances to the development of pharmaceuticals to reduce anxiety, seizures, and the speed with which dementias progress. We implant microprocessors into the brains of quadriplegics to help them move objects by means of robotic limbs, and into the brains of the blind to help them see.

Why would Mind Upload denaturalization form the single Rubicon we should never attempt to cross?

If *our* neurotechnologies teams don't risk that crossing, do we honestly believe others in less ethical and open nations would follow suit? The military applications alone are incalculable. For better or worse, we find ourselves at the brink of a neurotechnologies race that will no doubt make both the space and nuclear arms races seem downright quaint by comparison.

We also might address the critique by asking: Why *shouldn't* we aspire to an existence beyond the merely human, the merely *us* as we now understand that word? Can we honestly argue monkeys should never seek to become more-than-monkeys who can delight in art, science, literature, sports, and deep feeling, on the grounds that such higher pleasures are not monkey pleasures?

Follow such reasoning, and we would find ourselves tripping into the argument of the Reformation Government in the former United States, which holds certain educational or socioeconomic groups should not aspire to transcend *their* present conditions.

Certainly we can, so to speak, enjoy monkey pleasures as well as human, human as well as transhuman ones.

I would thereby contend that we are not so much losing as gaining choices. Being born a human is an accident of fate. We are in a position to change that. We have acquired fresh ways to expand our range of experiences and capabilities, gain greater insight, and participate more fully in every aspect of existence, in consciousness and embodiment, even in temporality itself.

Moreover, I insist that the last thing our species wants to do is cede control to the evolutionary being that will come after us. This leads us to a crucial survival argument. If we cannot modify our mental abilities as a species, then we are constrained to an evolutionary niche, and, if evolutionary history has taught us anything, it is that those niches almost always disappear ... and usually at the hands of a more powerful species.

With that said, let us return to the present. I should like to shift our attention to a different, admittedly intermittent species attribute: our embrace of social conscience.

The spread of totalitarian regimes has led to a refugee crisis heretofore unseen in history. As much as the NorAf-Euro Union has wanted to serve as sanctuary for those fleeing persecution and environmental wreckage, our own resources and infrastructure have over the past two decades been taxed to the breaking point.

It is in light of this that we have yet another, profoundly humanitarian reason to consider Mind Upload.

With great pleasure, let me introduce you to Josiah and Elisha Richardson. They first contacted me six weeks ago as this stage of our research neared completion. Before the suspension of the Constitution in the former United States, Josiah trained as a neuroscientist, joining the BRAIN Initiative team at Boston University. Elisha studied climatology and became associate professor at Wheaton College. With the establishment of the Reformation Government, they fell prey to one of the early Intellectual Ablutions and were forced into a re-education center in West Roxbury.

Upon their release, Josiah and Elisha spent the next three and a half decades in the business sector, working as tellers for the Evangelical Bank in New Jerusalem. With the latest round of Antisepsis designed—in the parlance of the Reformation Government—to cleanse the state of those living before 2035, thereby freeing up assets and further abbreviating the country's cultural memory—the Richardsons feared not only mistreatment based on their political beliefs, but also the horrors of public crucifixion.

With the help of the American Resistance, they breached the Reformation Government's firewall to contact the neurotechnologies center at Tunis University, about whose research they had read on the Delphian, that part of the Complexity, as most of you know, overseen by the American Resistance and intended to allow users to remain anonymous and untraceable.

Tunis University alerted us here in Cairo. An assessment was made to determine if the couple might be good candidates for inaugurating our RMU—Refugee Mind Upload—Project. After an evaluation taking into account the couple's asylum qualifications, medical standing, and likelihood of success, our consortium determined the Richardsons were superb pioneer subjects.

Seven days ago, the RMU Project became fully operational. Six days ago, at an undisclosed location, we commenced scanning Josiah and Elisha's brains. Late yesterday, we completed the data transfer. The former's mind, I am pleased to report, now resides safely in our quantum mainframe housed at the Libyan International Medical University, while the latter's nests at Uppsala University.

Please think about the sentence I just spoke: *The former's mind now resides safely in our quantum mainframe housed at the Libyan International al Medical University, while the latter's nests at Uppsala University.* Those words represent nothing less than the culmination of decades of labor. The RMU Project involved countless hours of collaborative research, false starts, dead ends, calibrations, recalibrations, conceptual and practical reboots, good old-fashioned guesswork, and thousands of tests that led us from studies in the 2010s on the freshwater hydra, whose tubular body barely reaches ten millimeters when fully extended, and which in place of a brain possesses a structurally simple nerve net, to chimpanzees, with whom we share ninety-six percent of our genome.

And here we are at long last.

It is not too much to say that, as we switched on the scanner that began the procedure last Monday, I felt as if our teams of researchers, computer scientists, neurosurgeons, neurotechnologists, and countless technicians were holding hands with Allah.

Let me just—there we go. You see to my left a holographic display of my console here at the Mind Emulation Studies Department at Cairo University. Floating above it you see a throw switch ghost. Run my hand through it, and the quantum mainframes in Tunis and Uppsala, which are in the process of booting even as I speak, will come fully alive. A few instants later, Josiah and Elisha will grow cognizant of the favorable outcome to their uploads, new states of being, successful refugee status, and, finally, your presence.

Please bear in mind it may take a few minutes for the couple to fully appreciate and assimilate the information they have become and begin to respond to their environments—that is to say, to communicate with us.

I kindly ask your patience.

It might be helpful to imagine what they will experience as something akin to one surfacing from anesthesia. Our resuscitation teams will need to help them orient, run a set of diagnostics, and, in all probability, effect several small software adjustments.

More difficult to navigate may be the precipitous shock of disembodiment, but we predict, given their full understanding of the procedure in advance, that they will adjust in relatively short order.

•

Enough with preliminaries. Let me conclude these remarks by under-scoring how deeply grateful I am to see your interest in the RMU Project. I want to thank you all again for joining us on this historic day to celebrate our consortium's success, for reporting to the greater world, and, in some cases, for considering the abundant investment opportunities.

This is a day that that little boy has been waiting for since he first picked up the science fiction novel about astronauts put into therapeutic hibernation on their thousand-year flight into the heart of our galaxy, and asked himself how he could become as timeless as they did.

Every once in a great while, a revolution comes to pass that literally changes everything. Writing, five thousand years ago, gave us the trans-generational accumulation of knowledge. The compass ignited the Age of Discovery. The printing press the Information Age. The internal combustion engine the Industrial Revolution. The light bulb transformed indoor living and the rhythms of urban spaces. Antibiotics and contraceptives. The telephone and TV. The atomic bomb and space flight. The computer, the internet, and genetic engineering.

Here we are again, ladies and gentlemen, at the threshold of the unimaginable.

And so, without further ado, let me introduce you to tomorrow today—in person: Josiah and Elisha Richardson.

Please help me count down.

Three ...

Two ...

One ...

And ...

:::: 29 :::: october :::: 2072 :::: 11:11 a.m.

why can't

why can't I

why can't I touch ha— ha—

her hand

her

why can't I touch her hand

why can't I touch her hand

why can't I touch her hand

why can't I touch her hand

why can't I touch her hand

why can't I touch her hand

why can't I touch her hand

why can't I touch her hand

why can't I touch her hand

why can't I touch her hand

why can't I touch her hand

why can't I touch her hand

why can't I touch her hand

why can't I touch her hand

why can't I touch her hand

why can't I touch her hand

why can't I touch her hand

why can't I touch her hand

why can't I touch her hand

why can't I touch her hand

why can't I touch her hand

why can't I touch her hand

why can't I touch her hand

why can't I touch her hand

why can't I touch her hand

why can't I touch her hand

why can't I touch her hand

why can't I touch her hand

why can't I touch her hand

why can't I touch her hand

her

why can't I touch her han

why an't I tou   her   an

wh   n't I tou   er   a

w   n't I   a

I   her

acknowledgments

The author wishes to thank Sandeep Bhagwati for the invitation to engage collaboratively with the Fukushima disaster for a performance at The House of World Cultures in Berlin, an undertaking which gave rise to the 11 March 2011 sequence; Dietmar Arnold and Sascha Keil from Berliner Unterwelten for the bunker tours, the books, and the information about the last hours of the Battle of Berlin in Humbolthain, which fed the 2 May 1945 sequence; the National Endowment for the Arts, the University of Utah Faculty Fellows Award, and a sabbatical from the University of Utah, all of which helped this novel become itself; *Big Other*, *Colorado Review*, *Conjunctions*, *The MacGuffin*, *Narrative Magazine*, and *Sulfur Surrealist Jungle*, in which excerpts from this novel first appeared in different forms; Lidia Yuknavitch for all the conversations we've shared over the decades in the Vesuvio of the mind; Melanie Rae Thon for the support, friendship, and love through the years in the City Creek of the heart; and Hacktorp as a state of being.